Gerrett D
said, "I a

Or at least that's what Libelle wished his words
were. What she'd often daydreamed he would say
before confessing his love and proposing marriage.
What he actually said was…well, she had no idea.
Mortification inched up her spine. She wasn't
going to ask him to repeat himself. Not when she
felt all warm and jittery and…

Oh, dear, was it him smelling of citrus and
sandalwood?

She eyed the cut of Gerrett's waistcoat again.
He wasn't as lean as she remembered, yet not
corpulent, either. Matured, yes, that was it.

At the sound of her name on his breath, she
sighed.

"You *are* Miss Liberty Adele Judd," she somehow
registered him saying.

"Yes," she answered. A joyful laugh bubbled
up from the tips of her toes, which was as
inconceivable as Gerrett Divine standing not five
feet away and there to see her. Her! Yet he was,
even though five years ago he'd vowed he never
wanted to see her again.

"Libelle," Ursula practically yelled as she jerked
on the bell sleeve of Liberty's gown. "The boy
said how sorry he was to have broken your heart.
Answer him."

GINA WELBORN

RWA-Faith, Hope & Love chapter president Gina Welborn worked in news radio, writing copy, until she had a stunning epiphany—the news of the day is rather depressing! Thus, she took up writing romances, because she loves happily ever after. She is an active member of ACFW and RWA and the author of three inspirational romance novellas. A moderately obsessive fan of *Battlestar Galactica, Community* and *Once Upon a Time,* Gina resides in a wee little town outside a larger (but not large) town in SW Oklahoma. Thanks to her pastor-husband's ability to spray a fabulous chemical called Demon, her children don't get to enjoy raising hunter spiders, grasshoppers and crickets. While they are (mostly) saddened, Gina is delighted.

GINA WELBORN

The Heiress's Courtship

HEARTSONG
PRESENTS

Recycling programs
for this product may
not exist in your area.

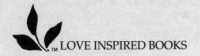 LOVE INSPIRED BOOKS

ISBN-13: 978-0-373-48689-2

THE HEIRESS'S COURTSHIP

Copyright © 2014 by Gina Welborn

www.Harlequin.com

Printed in U.S.A.

Love yet therefore the stranger:
for ye were strangers in the land of Egypt.
—*Deuteronomy* 10:19

For my mom, the seamstress

I never really understood how you could enjoy sewing until I started writing. The joy is in the creation as much as seeing someone enjoy the finished product. Thank you for letting me use your machine to sew the world's most atrocious Barbie clothes.

Chapter 1

Hillsdale, Michigan, February 1856

The Reverend Scott didn't even know he had ruined her life. He would, after Liberty Judd confronted him. In the meantime, she patiently listened to the engine's brakes screech to a halt at the Hillsdale station.

Her parents would be horrified to learn she'd sat on a burlap sack in a pitch-black railcar instead of on a seat in a private coach. The mail train's passenger car had been full. To return to Hillsdale tonight, her only option had been a seat in the baggage car—given only because she'd begged repeatedly and offered a more than generous price. She'd even been in too much of a hurry to take the time to change out of the olive-green ballgown she'd sewn specifically for her stepmother's fortieth birthday extravaganza. The same ball she *should* be enjoying instead of fleeing Chicago on the Southern Michigan Railroad's last eastbound train.

Not only did she likely smell of the smoke seeping through the car's wood-planked walls, but her gown and winter cloak were filthy, her pocketbook empty and her life miserable. At least she'd wisely exchanged her dancing slippers for woolen socks and sturdy winter boots before her preball escape.

The baggage car's center doors slid open with a harsh squeak, paining her already noise-weary ears, sending in an onslaught of wintry wind and snow flurries to bite at her face.

"Miss Judd," said the gravelly-voiced engineer, "you ready?"

"Yes, sir," Liberty said over the engine's clamor.

She stood and drew her fur-lined cloak's hood over her head, then stepped to the open doors. Steam from the churning engine billowed about. Under the glow of the gas lamps, she noticed the redness of the engineer's nose and cheeks, and she imagined she looked the same. Her face certainly felt cold.

"I am much obliged for the assistance." Like Cinderella returning home from the ball at midnight, she placed her leather-gloved hands in those of the engineer and the baggage-master. As they helped her down from the baggage car to the depot's snow-covered wooden platform, she added, "I'm sorry I put you even further behind schedule."

"The blizzard is the sole blame." The engineer's frown deepened. He touched the brim of his hat, muttered, "Evening," and walked toward the engine.

A heavy gust of snow blew across the platform. Her crinoline belled. Liberty shivered and drew her fur-lined cloak tighter across her chest. After hurrying into the stove-warmed telegraph office, she rested against the closed door. If she weren't still so angry at her parents *and* at the Reverend Scott, she'd fall to the ground and give in to the tears she'd fought during the slower-than-normal train ride. Only she wouldn't cry, because doing so would validate her parents' view that, fitting for her twenty-two years, she was "selfish and immature."

She felt her upper lip curl.

She'd spent too many years as their doormat. Time to pick herself up and walk—no, flee—away.

"Uhh, Miss Judd, why are you here at this hour?"

Liberty drew back her hood, sending snowflakes fluttering to the ground. Almost midnight!

"Charlie, I must send an immediate telegram," she said to the rotund telegrapher standing behind the counter. "Could I impose upon you to loan me the money until later?" She held up her beaded pocketbook. "I would leave this as collateral."

"Keep it, Miss Judd. Paying for your telegram is the least I can do considering you altered my suit again without charge."

"I insist upon a loan. The alteration was a gift."

"But I—" Clearly convinced by her I-insist look, his words broke off, and he picked up his pencil in preparation to write her message. Then he eyed her strangely. "Why are you wearing a tiara?"

She touched the diamond-and-emerald circlet her stepmother had inserted in her strawberry-blond hair, before Father informed her that she would *not* be returning to Hillsdale to finish the semester. Instead, the youngest member of his advisory board, Mr. Xavier Peabody, Esq., would propose to her at the ball, and she *would* accept.

Liberty lowered her hand and sighed.

"It's a wretched and tedious story." No one at the school or in the village, save for a select few, knew of her parents' wealth. She'd prefer to keep it that way. "The telegram needs to say, 'Back in Hillsdale. Will return in June per original agreement.'" *Unless I've figured out a way to live on my own without your interference.*

After giving her parents' names and address, she glanced at the frost-covered window. If she were staying in the ladies' dormitory instead of Bentzes' Boarding-house, she would have three times the distance to walk. Although, thinking of school—

She focused on Charlie and maintained as much calmness as she could despite the sinking feeling in her stomach. "Could you not tell Lady Principal Whipple of my midnight arrival?"

"Ahh, those dastardly deportment rules."

Seeing his grin, she smiled, too. "I have succeeded thus far in not breaking any. I would rather not begin tonight." *Or do anything to risk being expelled.*

The locomotive's whistle blew—a deep, guttural sound. A forlorn call in the night.

Liberty stepped to the window to watch the train ease out of the station. The vibrations under her feet increased along with the compounded chugging sound. She grabbed the window frame to hold steady.

One...two...three...

She continued to count as each boxcar slowly passed. From what she could tell, everyone in the lone passenger car was asleep. Not that she blamed them. The normal four-hour ride from Chicago to Hillsdale had taken almost twice as long tonight with nothing to watch sail by except snow.

Charlie then focused on a paper in his left hand while his right was poised over the iron telegraph. He started tapping. Likely he would first contact the Adrian depot, the next stop before Toledo, before sending her message.

Not wanting to disturb him, Liberty exited the telegraph office and released an immediate groan at the crisp wind. She hurried past the Freed family's carriage parked next to the depot, with their driver, Jonas, likely keeping warm inside. Was Dalton Freed finally returning home? Less concerned with gossip than with getting to a comforting fire, she dashed down the street. Her boots crunched on the snow, sinking several inches into what had accumulated throughout the evening, soaking the bottom flounce of her gown.

One more block and around the corner and she'd be at the boardinghouse.

No matter how dreadful she felt at the moment, life would have been worse had she never left *Chicago* four months ago. She didn't care about impressing everyone with the latest innovations from New York and London, or attending parties for the sole purpose of being seen, or pretending to enjoy the opera. *Always smile. Sit up straight. Eat the snails even if you don't like them.*

Artifice and pretense.

Thank the Lord she had never married Gerrett Divine. Life as his perfect society wife would have been suffocating. *Not* that he'd ever asked her to marry him. *Not* that he'd even cared that she'd loved him. She had, though. Faithfully. Desperately. Miserably. Wastedly.

With a sad chuckle, she turned the corner on the last block to the boardinghouse. Love should never make a person feel less. That's why she wasn't going back to Chicago and agreeing to her parents' demand. She'd find a way to support herself, to stay in college. After all, this was 1856, not 1756. The world was evolving, despite her parents' wishes, and like her roommate, Katie, she was joining that change.

Maybe she would open a sewing shop like Katie kept suggesting.

BOOM. At the sound of the explosion, Liberty jolted to a stop. Time seemed to stand still. A sliver of smoke snaked from the boardinghouse's chimney. Despite the

placidness of the immediate view, Liberty looked beyond
the boardinghouse. In the distance, in the direction of
the sound, a section of the charcoal night sky grew pink
and brighter.

Almost aflame.

That would be about where the railroad track curves—

She gasped, then darted across the street and into the
boardinghouse.

She slammed the door. "Ursula! Josef! Oh, Katie, there
you are! Why are you still up?"

Dr. Katie Clark stood from her seat at one of the four
dining hall tables. The anatomy students she was tutoring
stood, too. Doors throughout the boardinghouse opened
and slammed closed; stomping across the floor overhead
increased.

"Why are *you* back?" Katie asked with a what-have-
you-done-this-time gleam in her eyes. "You aren't supposed to return from Chicago until Sunday."

"Doesn't matter. Train wreck!"

Liberty and Katie arrived at the crash not long after the
explosion. Ash mixed with the falling snow and spreading
smoke. Eastbound and westbound passengers were exiting
the upright cars, some carrying children. Liberty forced
down her tears and wished her train had only tipped over,
instead of slamming into another engine.

She stayed in the six-passenger sleigh while Katie and
her study group climbed out. Until she had train wreck
victims to transport back to Hillsdale, she had nothing to
do but watch and pray.

Myriad sleighs and wagons pulled up next to them.

Katie, holding a lantern high, commanded the attention of those around her. "Spread out along the tracks.
We don't want to miss any victims who might have been
thrown free of the wreckage."

With a collective nod, the students fanned out.

Katie then looked over her shoulder at the village of Hillsdale in the distance. Her eyes closed.

Assuming she was praying, Liberty followed suit. *Help us save these people, Jesus. Help me not panic. Help Katie know exactly what to do, although I really don't know why I'm praying that because Katie always knows what to—*

At Katie's "hello," Liberty opened her eyes. Her roommate trudged through the snow toward the bungled cars of the westbound train. The cries from passengers grew with each passing moment. Men worked frantically to put out the fire in the eastbound mail car.

Her attention drew to a college student standing on the top of a passenger car lying on its side. George Quackenbush held a lantern while motioning to someone below. Soon he stepped back, and a man wearing a fur-trimmed greatcoat climbed through a side window. Once through, the man reached down, lifted out a crying child and gave it to George, then with his free hand, he helped the mother climb out. The man looked out over the wreckage, talking to the Quackenbush twin and never once focusing on where Liberty sat.

Still, the light from the lantern was enough to highlight his face for her to recognize him. To recognize Gerrett Divine.

Her hands shook, pulse raced. Not him. Not here. Not *now.*

With a groan Liberty dropped to the floorboard of the sleigh, hoping the wooden front would block her from his line of sight. Her lungs pressed tight. Her skin felt as aflame as the mail car. What was Gerrett doing here? Had he come for her? That made no sense. Not after the last words he'd said to her five years ago before leaving for his grand tour. He was returning home to Chicago with a bride to introduce to his parents and grandparents. A French heiress. Yes, her brother had told her that at Christmas.

Liberty peeked over the front of the sleigh for another look.

He wasn't even close enough for her to appreciate the color of his eyes, yet she remembered the exact shade: azure-blue. A hue perfectly matching the fraternity blazers Gerrett and her brother had worn when home on holiday. Some odd quickening inside chased away the chill from the snowy night, making her think of sunshine, sewing machines and crisp butter cookies—her favorite things.

As Gerrett had been…for far too many years of her life.

She sighed, as she had every time he'd visited the house to see her brother or had walked blindly past her at the opera or helped her father's Masonic lodge plant flowers in Lake Park. His extended European tour had done nothing but improve his powerful presence. His cheekbones were as well sculpted as she remembered, hair light brown, albeit tousled by the wreck. If anything, his bristled jaw only made him more dashing.

Gerrett Henry Divine IV. Heir to the vast Divine hotel, railroad and shipping fortune. The man was once *the* premier bachelor in Chicago society. She had spent six months practically fasting morning, noon and night for his return. Not that he'd cared. Took another six months of aimless daily walks around Lake Park before she gained enough clarity to realize she'd been a self-absorbed seventeen-year-old who laid all her hopes for happiness and significance at his well-shod, indifferent feet. That epiphany had led her into serving others through mission projects, which led her into attending church, which introduced her to Jesus.

Unrequited love wasn't all bad.

The cruel irony of it all! She had finally decided to

break free from her parents, to live life on her own, and the antithesis of all she'd become returns. For the rest of the night, as she aided the wounded and ministered to those in need, she would have to do everything she could to avoid the last man she ever wanted to see again.

All because he'd said she meant nothing to him.

All because he'd broken her heart.

All because—

She blinked at the horrid tears in her eyes. Because seeing him made her pine for what could have been *if* he had loved her. And that, truly, was the most pathetic reason of all.

"Liberty Adele Judd," she whispered, "it's time to put aside all childhood dreams and grow up."

Chapter 2

The train wreck was the least of his worries.

Cradling the injured child, Gerrett Divine stood at the front of the dwindling line of injured passengers in the Hillsdale's First Church foyer. The top of his head hurt. Ached, rather, like Martin Luther was nailing his *Ninety-Five Theses* to it. He wasn't too sure it had stopped bleeding, either. True, when the train he was on collided with the other, he'd hit his temple on the seat before him then on the window and ceiling as the car tilted and fell like a fractured snake, throwing him and everyone inside around like marbles.

Yet the burden on his heart ached more.

God, change my heart. I don't want to marry Ann, but I gave my word.

The woman in front of Gerrett moved into the sanctuary and sat in a nearby pew, and Gerrett stepped forward.

"I'm Reverend Burton Scott," said the wintry-bundled blond man holding an open journal. He couldn't be more than a day older than Gerrett. Smiling, he adjusted the spectacles on his nose even though they'd sat perfectly positioned. "I am sorry for the collision, but do know you will be well cared for while you are in Hillsdale. First questions are for you, and then the child. Name?"

"Gerrett Henry Divine. The fourth." He threw the latter in out of habit merely because his grandfather always insisted on the distinction.

"Age, employment and destination?"

"Twenty-seven years old. Architect. En route to my hometown of Chicago after a five-year absence. Traveling alone," he clarified even though the man hadn't asked.

The Reverend Scott gently touched the head of the boy Gerrett held. "Then whose child is this?"

The boy said nothing.

Gerrett answered, "I found him wandering—"

"No, but Dr. *Katie* Clark can!" a woman yelled from outside.

The Reverend Scott's gaze immediately shifted to the open doors.

Gerrett frowned at the sudden and odd sensation he felt. That voice— He knew it.

The reddish glow from the gas street lamps along the road illuminated the sparkle of the tiara in her hair. A strangely familiar young woman wearing the diamonds and emeralds moved so quickly the snow didn't have time to collect more than a dusting on the shoulders of her green velvet cloak. After drawing the fur-lined hood over her head, she pointed the injured and uninjured adults to the gray-bricked church where Gerrett was, standing, smiling a bit and staring at her.

He knew her.

Or at least he thought he did. She'd sounded familiar. She looked familiar. So why couldn't he remember her name? Or where he had seen her before? He felt rather dizzy. He took a step forward, then remembering the child he held, stopped. No sense chasing her down to find out how he knew her. But if she would meet his gaze, perhaps he could remember.

Only she didn't look his way, as if he didn't exist.

"The date?" the Reverend Scott ground out.

"Friday, the eighth of February," Gerrett added to the list of his verbal responses as he continued to watch her. That was the date, wasn't it?

"Mr. Divine?"

At the preacher's prompting—exactly an unpleasant slap on the arm—Gerrett reluctantly broke the connection he had with the woman and turned around. "I know that lady."

The Reverend Scott glared at him. Out of distrust, anger or even from jealousy, Gerrett wasn't sure. "What's her name?"

"I have no idea."

"Mr. Divine, I suggest—" his gaze shifted to Gerrett's aching forehead "—you find a spot on a pew to rest. Dr. Clark is currently seeing to the worst injuries. The child?"

True. He ought to rest. Gerrett shifted the boy in his arms. "His name is Samuel. Hasn't seen his parents since the collision. He's favoring his left shoulder."

Samuel sniffled and buried his head against the fur collar of Gerrett's woolen coat.

The Reverend Scott motioned at a pretty redhead carrying an armful of blankets, drawing an immediate smile from her. "Miss Wittingham, might we have your assistance?"

He was going to find out who the woman was and how he knew her.

Gerrett sipped his honeyed tea as Olive Wittingham sat on the other side of Samuel and questioned the boy, who quickly figured out how to earn more cookies by delaying his answers. To the hotel laundress's credit, she seemed to figure out his machinations by the fifth cookie. To the tea's credit, Gerrett no longer felt disjointed. In fact, he felt rather determined.

"Miss Wittingham?"

She stopped chuckling and looked from Samuel to him. "Yes, sir?"

"Earlier I saw a woman near your age, wearing a green cloak and a tiara. Might you know her?

Wariness flittered in her hazel eyes, but she then recovered with a renewed smile. "I'm not sure. What else did she look like?"

"Blond hair. Maybe red, but lighter than yours. Younger than I am. Her eyes are— I don't really know, but her cloak was green." He pointed to his head and repeated, "She had diamonds and emeralds in her hair and is so lovely, a man would yet look at her and never wish to stop."

Her head nodded as if she were processing all he'd admitted…and finding it too unrealistic to believe.

Could he have imagined her? After five years of living in France, that he would know someone in Hillsdale, Michigan, was as likely as— He couldn't fathom any possible odds. Gerrett stared at the remains of the tea in his cup. Somehow he knew in the depths of his soul that he had met the lady before. They had shared a dance. They had talked.

"I am not a romantic, Miss Wittingham," he said, looking to her. "But in an unexplainable way, I know the lady I saw matters to me."

"Smitten, are you?" Her question held not a hint of mocking. No, she seemed as contemplative as he.

Attracted, he was. But smitten? Even if he were— and he wasn't—he was a Divine. He knew what was expected of him. He had a soon-to-be fiancée waiting for him in Chicago. He wasn't about to become smitten with any woman no matter how familiar, or appealing, she was to him.

"Have you ever seen someone or something, and not being able to recall how you knew the person or thing plagued you?"

Miss Wittingham nodded.

"That woman plagues me."

"Oh." She cast a longing gaze across the noisy sanctuary to where the Reverend Scott spoke with an elderly couple. "Did you ask *him* for her name?"

"No. I suspect he wouldn't have told me if I had."

"True," she muttered. "Not if he suspected you had any interest in her." She turned back to face Gerrett.

Little Samuel looked up at him with as much curiosity as Miss Wittingham, who didn't say anything more for several moments.

Then she whispered, "Silver."

"Silver?"

She leaned forward yet still spoke softly. "Mr. Divine, her eyes are a light blue-gray. Silvery."

For a moment Gerrett couldn't do anything but stare at the young woman. "You know her?" he asked just as softly, even though he had no idea why they were whispering.

She nodded.

"Is she—" Gerrett paused because he felt a peculiar sense of dread "—married?"

Miss Wittingham's sudden laugh drew the attention of everyone in the sanctuary, including a mousy-haired nurse. "Liberty married? Good gracious, have you any idea who her parents are?"

Liberty?

Gerrett shifted on the pew that seemed harder, more

unwelcoming. He had only ever known one Liberty, but the spoiled heiress she was would have no business in Hillsdale. Still, he had to ask.

"Liberty," he said with a sour taste in his mouth, "as in Liberty Judd from Chicago? Younger sister to Leonidas Judd and Lurana Judd Templeton? Daughter to Edward and Caroline Judd?" *Say no.*

She nodded.

Gerrett held back the first curse he'd ever thought about uttering since returning to his faith in Christ a year ago. He could still remember how she'd gripped his hands, begging him to love her. Nausea and shame at how he'd responded churned the tea in his stomach.

"Sir," Samuel said between bites of his last cookie, "are you going to get sick? There's a bucket by the altar."

"I agree," Miss Wittingham said. "You don't look well. I can ask Dr. Clark to examine you now."

The last time he'd seen Liberty don't-forget-my-middle-name Adele Judd, melon, not hourglass, described her figure. Unflattering, short, carrot-colored curls framed her face. As many red-and-white-striped ruffles as blue bows bedecked the gown the annoying girl had designed and sewn for the Independence Day festival. The only reason he'd danced with her was because her brother had asked him to.

Once he realized he was shaking his head, he stopped. That lovely nymph he'd seen amid the snow could *not* have been Liberty Judd. Unless…the ugly duckling had actually grown into a swan.

Unable to hear anything except the pounding of his pulse, Gerrett leaned forward on the pew, rested his elbows on his knees and gripped his forehead that seemed to ache more than it had since the collision.

What were the statistical chances that after five years, he (1) would be returning home to Chicago to propose to one of his closest friends, when (2) a train wreck would strand him in a village of less than two thousand people, where (3) he would see a distractingly beautiful woman, who (4) just so happened to be the last person on earth he would ever want to see again? Coincidence? Providential joke? He couldn't fathom any possible odds for the irony of it all.

Why now, Lord? She made my life miserable.

He let out a resigned breath. He didn't have to hear God's answer to know the reason why he was here. His shame told him why.

Because Liberty Judd had offered her love and he had callously tossed it back, unwanted.

Because he'd wanted to break her heart. And he had.

Finally, because he was a Divine, and Divines always made right what they wronged. Thus, come morning, he would find Miss Judd. And then he would make amends.

No matter how humiliating it was.

Chapter 3

"Do you realize how you have ruined my life?"

Liberty watched Burton Scott shift awkwardly at the two-person kitchen table where the Bentzes shared their meals. True, she could've had this conversation out in the dining hall. But with the Friday classes canceled and boardinghouse residents lingering about, the only place to have a private conversation was in the kitchen.

Of course, Hillsdale's deportment rules necessitated a chaperone.

Thus she sat across from the still-silent reverend while Ursula Bentz washed the breakfast dishes. The thirty minutes following breakfast cleanup was Ursula's customary moment to study Scripture and have honest conversation with the Lord. But with the boardinghouse overfilled with extra guests because of the train wreck, lunch preparations had to begin sooner. Not that Ursula had given the ham on the counter the briefest of glances. Or the basket of potatoes needing to be peeled, or onions, carrots and beets to be chopped for the stew that was to be served with the rye bread rising near the hearth.

No, she seemed content with listening to Liberty have an *honest conversation* with the good reverend.

While Liberty had no desire to hurt or embarrass the Reverend Scott, he needed to hear the truth, and since he wasn't speaking, the weight of the conversation fell to her. This only added to her vexation.

Time to be forthright.

"The letter you sent my parents, it... Well, their standards limit who they will allow to— You aren't *wealthy enough for them*." With a frustrated sigh, Liberty rested her hands in the lap of her gold paisley gown. This rejection of his courtship wasn't going as smoothly as she'd planned earlier this morning. "Why did you send them a letter asking permission to court me? I have not given you—or anyone—any indication that I wish to marry."

He leaned forward, resting his arms on the table, his hands stretched out to her. "Miss Judd, when I first saw you, I *knew*."

"You *knew* what?"

"That you were the one."

"The one?"

"For me."

"For you?"

"You're a God-given blessing." He cocked his head. Raised his blond brows. Smiled in a manner that had caused many of Liberty's fellow college girls to giggle and swoon. Had she ever seen whiter and more even teeth? Was there a primer male specimen in Hillsdale? Even his spectacles added to his charm. Yet she felt nothing.

Not even an ounce of attraction to him.

"My dear Miss Judd, even though we have only known each other these four months since you've been in Hillsdale, the connection we have...it's as if we've known each

other forever. The first time I saw you step off the train—
It was Thursday, October 2, and exactly at 12:23 p.m. my
world spun. Love does that."

"How precise your memory is," Ursula said in an impressed tone, yet her German accent sounded thicker than
usual. She grabbed another mixing bowl to dry. "Young
man, what is this spin you speak of? Like gravity? Or too
much sauerkraut?"

With a determined gleam in his eyes, Burton Scott
stood. He cleared his throat.

Oh, dear. Liberty eased to the edge of her seat. She
glanced between him and the kitchen door, calculating
how quick she could make her escape, if need be. Somehow the conversation had done its own love spin out of
her control.

"'As soon as I had seen her,'" he said, with a hand over
his heart, "'I was lost. For Beauty's wound is sharper than
any weapon's, and it runs through the eyes down to the
soul. It is through the eye that love's wound passes, and I
now became a prey to a host of emotions.'"

Ursula uttered a well-drawn out "Ahhhh. Shakespeare."

"No, ma'am. A Greek playwright my grandfather has
quoted for years. It's our family motto."

Liberty resisted the urge to roll her eyes. Burton Scott
had no fault to his name, character or appearance that she
knew of, save his obliviousness to the love Olive Wittingham had for him…and his besotted "host of emotions" for *her*.

"Love doesn't happen like that," she remarked. "In an
instant. At least for most people." When had she grown
so cynical about love?

To his credit, he didn't argue.

Instead, he knelt before her, clasping her hands between his. "I love you, Liberty Judd. You are my everything. Will you marry me?"

She looked away from him to Ursula, who was drying the last mixing bowl. While Ursula wasn't smiling, it was obvious that she was amused by the sudden proposal.

Only Liberty wasn't amused. Why wasn't she? Marriage would be an escape from the life her parents demanded of her, and Burton Scott believed in women being educated. While he didn't have the minimum wealth her parents would approve of, he wasn't poor. If she married him, she could stay at Hillsdale and earn her degree. She should be rejoicing, screaming, dancing and running into his embrace.

Why couldn't she feel something—anything—for the besotted reverend? It had to be because Gerrett had broken her heart so that she felt nothing anymore.

"I am not in love with you," she muttered.

"You could be, if you tried. Try, Miss Judd," he begged. "Open your heart to love me."

Was loving someone *that* easy? Decide to do it and it happened?

She'd loved Gerrett Divine for too many excruciating years and had finally stopped. Love shouldn't be something one could put on or take off as easily as a coat. It had to be more than a feeling of desire. It had to be… It was… What was more than a feeling? Did love consume a person? Or did it make a person live beyond herself? Did love take effort, or was it effortless? Selfish? Or selfless? Could it be both? Was it more than both?

She didn't know.

Burton Scott's fingers caressed hers. "My life is not complete without you."

Please love me, Gerrett. My life is not complete without you.

Her breath fled from her lungs.

"I'm sorry. No, I won't marry you." Liberty withdrew her hands and eased away from the table, away from him.

She didn't want him to hate or scorn her. At least not forever. Only long enough to kill the temporal idea he held that she was *the one* for him. Then in a stronger voice, she said, "Your life does not need me for it to be complete. I can't— No woman should be made to feel as if a man's completeness depended on her. You should probably go."

He stood.

After a nod toward Ursula, he left the kitchen.

An hour later Liberty had a cobbler baking in the hearth and was working on two others when Ursula finished cleaning the kitchen, stood next to Liberty and broke the uncomfortable silence.

"You are persnickety."

"No, I'm not," she answered with fervor in hopes of convincing Ursula, who now examined the basket-weave strips atop the next cobbler to be baked. Every second of silence increased the foreboding of a lecture that Liberty felt.

Ursula, to whom in the past four months she'd grown closer than her own stepmother, checked her watch and frowned. She then returned it to the pocket of the apron she wore over the new calico gown Liberty had sewn for her last week. After placing the lid on the Dutch oven, she carried it to the hearth. That she wore no crinolines left fire-tending duties to her. Yet she did nothing but stand there, holding the Dutch oven.

After a good minute, Ursula said, "Through an entire barrel of apples sort you will find the one that suits you best," she said, looking less sympathetic and more perturbed. "In every gown you sew, precise is your last stitch to first. Good enough is not in your nature."

"I am barely making a C in history, and I'm content with that."

"Because you care nothing of subject matter."

Liberty didn't counter Ursula's words. She couldn't. History bored her. So did many of her courses. In fact, the only reason she took classes at Hillsdale was because doing so had given her an excuse to leave Chicago. Not that she would admit that to anyone.

"So be it, but there's nothing wrong with being selective." Liberty punctuated her words with a smile.

Ursula deftly removed from the hearth the Dutch oven with the peach cobbler inside. After setting it atop the cast-iron cookstove, the stately boardinghouse owner hung the second Dutch oven over the fire. She then folded the towel in her hand as she walked back to Liberty.

"No amount of praying to the Lord this morning has lessened my frustration with you."

"Why be frustrated with me?"

Ursula slapped the towel down on the counter. "Because you are determined not to marry solely because your parents are determined that you do."

Liberty opened her mouth to contradict Ursula.

"Shh, *mein liebes kind.*" She muttered something indistinguishable under her breath. "In four months you've lived under my care, I have noticed every man who has shown you interest. Them all you discourage. Ayden Goswell—"

"Is my professor," Liberty interrupted. How many times did she need to remind Ursula of this?

"Twice a week he comes here for supper."

"During which he tutors me."

Once, she'd imagined what it'd be like having romantic feelings for Professor Goswell. Not only did he have a warm smile and an engaging manner, he was honorable, intelligent and passionate about teaching. Any woman he loved would have to share his enthusiasm for learning, reading, studying, history, books and sports. Liberty grimaced.

"Professor Goswell is currently courting Charmaine

Finney," she clarified, "and I like her very much. Besides, I could never love a man who spends his leisure reading *The Odyssey* and considers fencing a necessary fighting skill. Fencing, really?"

Ursula didn't look convinced. Actually, she looked, well, rather smug. Like her hypothesis had been confirmed, which made Liberty feel like the troll she looked like next to the Philistine-size woman.

"There is the coppersmith—"

"Mr. Emery? I alter his clothes while listening to him bemoan the fact that the woman he proposed to two years ago still hasn't given him an answer." Liberty gave an incredulous shake of her head. "Seriously, John Emery, a suitor? He doesn't like any types of berries. Says they taste seedy. Imagine! See, now that's persnickety."

"Sheriff Dawes does not come here for food."

"Rand Dawes only talks to me because he is interested in Katie."

That smug grin on Ursula's face increased in size. "Every day in January, in hopes his suit you'd favor, George Quackenbush walked you to—"

"Fred."

Ursula suddenly looked over her shoulder. "There is no Fred here."

"Uhh, Fred, not George—" Liberty smiled regretfully "—walked me to class. He's the shorter of the two." Or at least she thought he was.

"No, *libelle,* George did."

"Truly was Fred." Of course, he did give her odd looks when she called him by his given name, which probably wasn't his name now that she thought about it. Why did twins have to look so identical? "Fred," she repeated with a little less confidence in her tone.

Ursula rested her hands on her hips, her eyes never

leaving Liberty's face. "Can you still not tell those boys apart?"

Although the Quackenbush twins lived a floor above her in the boardinghouse, after four months of speaking to the twins every day, she still couldn't distinguish a difference in them.

Letting out an irritated snort, Liberty dusted the flour off the bodice of her apron. "It's not persnickety to wish to court a man and not continually wonder if he were himself or his twin brother. Truly. Were Fred—"

Ursula's brows rose.

"Fine," Liberty muttered testily. "Were *George* to have kissed me, I would have been mortified to ask him what his name was."

Her lips parted with surprise, and then Ursula laughed. Bellowed, actually.

Liberty crossed her arms, stared at the wood-beamed ceiling and patiently waited for her surrogate mother to regain composure.

Ursula dried her eyes with her towel. "Now, pray tell, what fault find you with the Reverend Scott?" When Liberty didn't answer immediately, Ursula repeated, *"With the Reverend Scott?* Because of you, the poor boy has a broken heart."

Liberty picked at the uneven edge of the dough she'd rolled.

"It wouldn't have worked," she mumbled. If only she could think of a way to transfer the Reverend Scott's devotion from her to Olive. Yet part of her—and she hated to admit it—liked feeling loved, liked receiving poetry and flowers, liked knowing when she walked into a room, one man saw only her.

"I'm not persnickety." She gave a little shrug. "I'm merely waiting for the best man, and Burton Scott isn't that. For me."

Ursula's brown, braided head slowly shook. "I doubt that. Through the front door of this boardinghouse *this* very moment, the perfect suitor could walk and you would not be bothered."

The image of Gerrett Divine standing atop the train car flashed in her mind. She'd fallen asleep last night imagining him climbing down the car and traversing the shin-deep snow to capture her in an embrace. *I've searched the globe,* he'd said, *and here you are.* Then he kissed her. She shivered at the memory.

No! Good gracious, no!

She was tired of aching for him. Tired of comparing all men to him.

She was finished with Gerrett Divine and unrequited love.

With a growl under her breath, she wiped away the traitorous goose bumps on her arms. Eventually she'd find a man who loved her with the devotion Burton Scott did.

"Oh, Ursula, I'd be bothered, all right." Liberty forced a chuckle even though she was feeling more offended, less amused and a bit sad. "I have cobblers to bake and potatoes to peel." With the sweetness of the baked cobbler filling the air, she quickly floured her rolling pin and resumed rolling even though the dough was at the correct thickness. "Besides, the likelihood of my ideal man being here in Hillsdale at this very moment is—"

Ursula inserted a butter knife in the center of the dough, hindering Liberty from any more rolling. Her voice grew tender. "Your parents desire the best for you."

She held back a scoffing response. Her parents desired the best for the family's reputation, especially how the marriage increased the family's wealth. Her interests were inconsequential, as her brother's had been, as her sister's had been. And now Leonidas and Lurana were shadows of their former childhood selves. Judd family mannequins. Expected to have as much personality, individual thought and voice as the wirework mannequin upstairs in the suite she shared with Katie.

She was not going to become like them.

"I am of age to make my own decisions."

"A wise man listens to his elders."

"My parents don't advise—they demand." Liberty set the rolling pin aside then wiped her cheek with the back of her flour-covered hand. "They always demand I do what they want regardless of my feelings. The only time my stepmother has ever listened to me was when I admitted feelings for my brother's closest friend. What mattered wasn't who I loved but how she could make a Judd-Divine wedding the social event of the decade." The bitterness of her words made her mouth feel like she cleaned her teeth with dirt.

Ursula cut strips for the lattice-top crust. She laid them in the third Dutch oven, atop summer-canned blackberries this time, until they were all uniform. When she looked up, she cradled her calloused palm around Liberty's peachy-pink one, pulling it to her ample chest.

"Do you not want to marry?" Her gentle words flew like an arrow into Liberty's heart.

Oh, how she yearned for a husband and babies and a house with a wraparound porch. That's all she wanted. That's all she had *ever* wanted. Well, that and to have it with Gerrett Divine. And now he was here. In Hillsdale. Avoiding him last night was the most difficult thing she'd ever done. Partially because she was still embarrassed over her behavior five years ago, but mostly because she feared talking to him—being near him—would resurrect her obsessive feelings for him.

She swallowed to ease the dryness of her throat.

"Yes." She gave Ursula's hand a squeeze. "Is it wrong

for me to not want to marry when the only reason I have for marrying right now is to escape my parents' clutches?"

"*Nein,* it is not."

"The man my parents have chosen for me to marry, Mr. Peabody, is a younger version of Father." Her voice caught, and for a moment she thought she might cry. "Sometimes I don't even like my parents. Most of the time, actually. How do I honor them when doing so means I lose any sense of *me?*"

The kitchen door opened enough for Ursula's husband, Josef, to lean inside. His brow and eyes were so wrinkled from squinting in the sun that it was difficult to distinguish whether he was concerned, excited or apathetic.

"Ursula?" he said in a tone that was as vague as his expression.

"*Ja?*"

"A gentleman is wishing to speak to Miss Liberty."

Before Ursula or Liberty could respond, the door opened wider, and Gerrett Divine walked into the room and said—

"I am sorry I broke your heart."

Or at least that's what Liberty thought his words were. What she'd often daydreamed he would say before confessing his love and proposing marriage. What he actually said was… Well, she had no idea. Mortification inched up her spine. She wasn't going to ask him to repeat himself. Not when she felt all warm and jittery and…

Oh, dear, was it he smelling of citrus and sandalwood?

Unable—*unwilling*—to meet Gerrett's gaze, Liberty focused on his clothes. He cut a dashing figure, which didn't help her to not think about him or about the annoying fluttering under her breastbone. His ebony frock coat with its wide, velvet collar and turned-up sleeves set off his brown-and-black-checkered trousers. His ivory shawl-collared waistcoat had a bold scroll pattern in a lighter thread—the cut of the vest a style she hadn't yet seen in Hillsdale or Chicago. What she'd give to remove his vest and trace a pattern. Remembering the silks that had arrived in the mercantile last month—why, she could probably have a dozen waistcoats in several sizes made by the end of next week!

Once she finished helping Ursula this morning, she was going to find Katie and get her advice on how to open a sewing shop.

She eyed the cut of Gerrett's waistcoat again. He wasn't as lean as she remembered, yet not corpulent, either. Matured, yes, that was it.

At the sound of her name on his breath, she sighed.

"You *are* Miss Liberty Adele Judd," she somehow registered him saying.

"Yes," she answered. A joyful laugh bubbled up from the tips of her toes, which was *as* inconceivable as Gerrett Divine standing not five feet away and there to see her. Her! Yet he was, even though five years ago he'd vowed he never wanted to see her again.

She pinched the inside of her left wrist until the pain brought her to her senses. She was not going to obsess over him anymore, for doing so was foolish, childish and pointless-ish. She groaned inwardly. Pointless. Adjectives aside, what mattered was she was *not* obsessing over this man anymore. And that was that.

"Libelle," Ursula practically yelled as she jerked on the bell sleeve of Liberty's gown. "The boy said sorry he was to have broken your heart. Answer him."

Chapter 4

Gerrett watched Miss Judd stare blankly at him. Her strawberry-blond hair was tiara-free and pinned in a serviceable bun at the nape of her neck. While he was no expert on fashion, her gold paisley gown well accentuated her figure and coloring.

"Miss Judd," he said, "I cannot return home without apologizing for how I spoke to you five years ago. I was a callous, inconsiderate, arrogant fool. My thoughts were of myself and living life for myself, regardless of whom I hurt, and I hurt you. Will you forgive me?"

His chest tightened in expectation of the chastisement and hate he deserved.

For a long moment she didn't move, didn't speak and didn't blink. She was staring at him as if she were seeing him—*really seeing him*—for the first time.

"Why now?" she finally asked in a voice so melodic that he instantly imagined children begging her to read them bedtime stories.

Gerrett wiped the moisture on his forehead, caused by the heat from the hearth and his own nervousness. This groveling wasn't going as smoothly as he'd planned over breakfast at the hotel. He had no right to ask for her forgiveness. If she really knew him, she would shake her head in disgust and run away. His mistreatment of her was one of his many sins.

You are forgiven.

He was.

Thank You, Lord, for the reminder.

Gerrett drew in some grace-filled air and released the shame he'd been clinging to. He then squared his shoulders. He wasn't responsible for how Miss Judd responded. His duty was to admit his wrong, offer grace even if none was given him and be at peace knowing he had done what God asked of him.

"Miss Judd, I deeply regret my mistreatment of you, and I understand if you are unable to grant forgiveness. I hold nothing against you."

After a shake to her head, she closed her eyes and touched the spot between her brows.

"Libelle," Ursula said with another tug on Miss Judd's sleeve, "answer the gentleman."

"This isn't how it's supposed to be," Liberty muttered under her breath.

"Excuse me?" and "What?" came from the other two in the kitchen.

Liberty gripped the edge of the counter. Her heart was racing as fast as her thoughts. She didn't have the answer. Facing the man she'd loved since the summer of her fifteenth birthday, and listening to him apologize for breaking her heart, she was overwhelmed. Her romantic dreams and the emotional wounds she'd nursed over the past five years faded into—well, into what, she wasn't sure.

She felt rather dizzy—vertiginous, to be specific. A happy, scared, confused, unable-to-breathe-or-flee-from-the-room feeling, not how she'd ever anticipated talking to him again would be. Even after the chaos following a train collision in the middle of the night somewhere along the four-mile stretch of land between Hillsdale and Osseo, Michigan. Even after he apologized for breaking her heart.

Something in her was different in this moment. She wanted to forgive him.

I do, Jesus, but I'm so afraid doing so will open my heart up to more hurt.

But neither did she want to be hard and unable to love.

Liberty looked to Ursula, who frowned as if she was equally confused. "I—I don't know what to answer."

"*Ja,* that is to be expected." Ursula smiled softly, brushed Liberty's cheek, whispered, "Flour," then checked the pocket watch she carried in her apron. "I'll see if anyone in the dining hall needs something. You must sort things out."

"Wait, Ursula!" She didn't want to be alone with Gerrett. She couldn't be. Hillsdale's rules for deportment clearly specified— "I can only receive gentleman callers in the parlor from 3:00 to 7:00 p.m." Merely thinking of Gerrett as a gentleman caller made her twitch.

"I will return shortly."

"But Principal Whipple—"

"Is not here and will not know. Worry not."

As Ursula walked to the kitchen door, Liberty watched, her eyes trailing the other woman until they rested on Gerrett. Smile lines curved around his mouth even when he wasn't openly smiling. Joy radiated from him. Why not? His parents adored him. He didn't carry the burden of never living up to their expectations. He wasn't a disappointment.

Of course not. He was a Divine.

She sighed. What made it worse, he, with that jaunty grin on his face, stood there all peaceful and serene despite not receiving her acceptance of his apology. He'd even found somewhere to shave and clean up from last night's train wreck—

"You have a bruise."

He looked at his hands. "Where?"

Wiping her hands on her apron, she hurried forward. She stopped in front of him and pointed gingerly toward the right side of his forehead, near the discolored place the size of a walnut.

He touched the knot and winced. "Oh, that. I hit my head when the railcar tipped."

"Did you see a doctor?"

"I saw several," he quipped. "There's, what, seven or eight in this village?" Then he smiled like a schoolboy proud of the answer he'd given his tutor.

Liberty growled. She grabbed his wrist and dragged him to the two-person table, and didn't ponder how ironic it was that an hour earlier she'd been in this very spot rejecting Burton Scott's ardent proposal. She'd had to break his heart, or at least break the romantic illusion his mind had created. Just as Gerrett had done to her.

She blinked over the stunning reality of it all.

It wouldn't have mattered if Gerrett had been considerate as she had tried to be to the Reverend Scott, or calloused as he had been to her all those years ago. Her reaction would have included as much pleading for him to love her as the Reverend Scott's had.

She pointed to a chair. "Sit," she ordered, and he obeyed. "Stay here while I go find my roommate, Katie. She's a doctor."

Liberty started to the door then stopped.

This was probably the last time they would ever speak to one another. He would continue on to Chicago. She would continue on with life in Hillsdale. With Ursula not in the room, she could say things she would never admit with an audience. Of course, she would have to do it quickly before Ursula returned.

Liberty looked to a snow-covered window, desperate to steady the frantic beating of her heart. Yet the intoxicating smell of him—citrus and sandalwood—she couldn't escape, and it hurt. Would she ever stop feeling this fluttering inside? Like little bursts of flavor in her mouth from eating freshly picked berries. Only the bursts were all throughout her body. After all the cruelty he'd said to her, she still felt drawn to him. She should hate him. Yet she'd give anything to kiss him and have him kiss her back.

And she yearned to scream her frustration.

"Miss Judd, I will take no offense to anything you say to me."

His words drew her gaze back to him, and she could just drown right there in his eyes as blue as Lake Superior in paintings.

Oh, Jesus, help me, because I want something more than this consuming desire I have for Gerrett. It hurts. It won't stop. I need You to stop it.

She had to speak to him. For her.

Expunge her feelings, and maybe then she could finally cut the emotional strings tying her to him. Thus she sat in the opposite chair. *Say it and be done,* she thought, smoothing the lap of her skirt.

"The six months after you left for France, I cried for you. I couldn't eat or sleep. Then I hated you."

She paused long enough to wonder if she was being too open.

"Once the grief and resentment passed, I clung to the hope of *someday.* After all, the basic nature of love is that it should be reciprocated—I love you, ergo you must love me, too. When it isn't, as William Congreve penned, 'Heaven has no rage like love to hatred turned—'"

"'Nor hell a fury like a woman scorned,'" Gerrett finished.

Liberty released a sad chuckle. Of all the quotes to remember from her dull literature class.

He didn't add more, as if he knew she wasn't finished with her confession.

"As I look back to that time," she admitted, "I ask myself, how did loving you make me a better person? It didn't. Loving you made me miserable. Wanting you made me equally miserable because I'd made you the center of my life. I believed that you could give me everything I needed, that you could give purpose to my life."

He studied her intensely. As if he were examining her soul to determine if she spoke truthfully, yet he didn't seem shocked at deciding she was. "Go on."

"I was an embarrassment to myself, my family. You. For that, I am deeply sorry."

He offered his hand to her. "All is well between us?"

Nodding, she placed her hand in his. His mesmerizing eyes remained fixed on her face. Where his hand tenderly held hers radiated with warmth. She yearned to be close to him. She wanted to cleave, which had to be one of the silliest words she'd ever heard the Reverend Scott preach in a sermon. Yet her lips parted, and she leaned in, her skin tingling. This feeling—this strange, wonderful, breathtaking feeling—was…one-sided, as it had always been.

She had to stop feeling this way.

Liberty released his hand and forced cheerfulness into her tone. "It is nice to put our pasts behind us."

"Freeing." He touched his bruised temple and winced again.

She regarded him a bit more closely. "Did a doctor examine you at all after the wreck?"

His gaze shifted to the side, brow furrowing as he clearly thought about last night's events. "Dr. Clark's nurse told me she would examine my injury after I finished my tea, but she never came back. So I left the church and took a room at the hotel. Slept a few hours, ate breakfast and then went in search of you."

"No one has looked at your head?"

"I'm fine. I wiped the matted blood out of my hair this morning."

Liberty stepped to his side. "Let me take a look." She gently shifted his light brown hair as she searched his scalp for more bruising. "My nursing skills are rather limited, but my roommate, Katie, enjoys discussing proper wound care. There's still a lot of dried blood, which means you have a gash some—" she gripped his shoulder to steady herself "—where. Needs wash…ing." Her eyes blurred, body wobbled. The noises in the room sounded as if she were underwater.

She was going to faint, and she could do nothing to stop it.

At the moment he carried the unconscious Miss Judd from the warm kitchen and into the half-full dining hall, Gerrett couldn't have cared less about the number of gazes upon them. She was so petite that he suspected a fair portion of the weight he carried was from her gown and petticoats.

"Mrs. Bentz," he called out. "She fainted."

She tossed the towel she held onto the dining table. "Into the parlor," she ordered, pointing to the foyer and hurrying that direction.

Gerrett followed her into the carpeted room. Once Miss Judd woke, she'd thank him for catching her before she earned her own gashed scalp.

"Here," Mrs. Bentz said, moving a pile of quilts off the settee.

Gerrett laid Miss Judd on the velvet cushions. Sitting on the edge, he reached to brush hair off her face before realizing not a single strand had loosened. He smoothed the silky red-gold hair anyway, even though Mrs. Bentz was watching him. Something besides his breaking of her heart had changed Miss Judd from the annoying girl he'd known.

He liked her openness. He liked her smell, like that of food and home. He liked her voice, her eyes, her touch. *Her.*

Gerrett scrambled to his feet and away from the settee to where Mrs. Bentz stood, still holding the armful of quilts. His pulse skittered with panic. He needed to leave. He needed distance.

Miss Judd's lashes fluttered. Her silver-blue eyes glanced about the room then focused on him and Mrs. Bentz. "I shouldn't have looked at your scalp. Blood makes me—"

Mrs. Bentz cleared her throat.

Miss Judd offered an apologetic shrug.

"I should go." Gerrett took a step toward the open parlor doors. "I need to see if there is a stage running and— Uhh, good day, Miss Judd. Any words you wish to pass along to your family? To your brother? I would be honored to bear them for you."

Alarm flittered across her features. "My family? I… Ahh, no need to tell them you saw me. Even Leonidas." She stood, and Gerrett resisted the urge to steady her until he was sure she wouldn't faint again. Miss Judd stepped forward, reaching a hand to the older woman. "Mrs. Bentz, would you join me in praying for Mr. Divine?"

"Ja." She replaced the quilts on the settee.

They joined hands then took his. Mrs. Bentz spoke

first, then Miss Judd began her prayer with asking a blessing over his health.

"You know my heart, Jesus," she said softly. "I beg You to lead Mr. Divine to the future You've prepared for him. Help us to aid him in his travels, as we also give aid to others stranded by the collision."

Whatever else she prayed, he did not hear. The pounding in his chest drowned out everything as he stared at her. Openly. Unashamedly. Her words weren't clichéd recitations. She spoke with the ease and confidence of someone who had an intimacy with Christ. She was someone who knew how to come boldly before the throne of grace to find mercy and grace in time of need. And he knew the answer to what else besides his breaking of her heart had changed Miss Judd—Jesus.

God had become the center of her life.

He'd been a believer since he was nine, yet he hadn't learned to be a disciple, to exercise his faith, to come boldly in prayer, until a year ago. And he was still learning. Last month Leonidas Judd had mocked his faith after he'd shared his decision to leave architecture, return to Chicago and take over the family company because he believed doing so was God's will. Leonidas had even mocked his desire to marry a woman whose first passion was Jesus, before going silent after Gerrett confessed who he was returning to Chicago to propose to.

Ann Bartlett.

He and Leonidas had known her since their youth. He liked Ann. Marrying her made good business sense. His parents wanted it, not that they'd demanded. As the sole Divine heir, his duty was to his family. If he couldn't leave a legacy with the buildings he designed, then he would through his children.

Miss Judd's grip on his hand tightened. Then it eased

so quickly he doubted it'd happened. "I ask all these things in You, through You and because of You, Jesus. Amen."

"Amen," Gerrett said in unison with Mrs. Bentz.

Without a final glance in his direction, Miss Judd let go of his hand and slipped out of the parlor, which immediately seemed less warm. Less vibrating with life. Less everything.

The boardinghouse owner motioned to the front doors. "Mr. Divine, shall we?"

Chapter 5

Gerrett grabbed his greatcoat from the coatrack next to the front door. He walked with Mrs. Bentz onto the wooden porch circling the boardinghouse. Having finished sweeping the snow from the roof, her husband now shoveled snow from the walk leading from the house to the carriage house, the wooden shovel occasionally scraping against the bricked path.

She closed the door behind him. "How do you know our Liberty?" She rested her back against the boardinghouse's door.

As the wintry air nipped at his cheeks and nose, Gerrett shrugged on his coat. "Her older brother is my closest friend. Five years ago, she had a *tendre* for me, and I—"

"What is *tondrah?*"

"It's French for tender feelings. Fondness."

"Ahh, love." Mrs. Bentz nodded slowly, stopped, then her wide mouth pursed and her brows drew together, causing a deep vertical crease. "Did she expect you to reciprocate her feelings?"

He nodded.

"Did you?"

"I broke her heart," he admitted over the continued scrape of Mr. Bentz's wooden shovel against the bricked sidewalk. "By some strange bit of Providence, I saw her again after all these years, and I knew this was my opportunity to make amends for the hurtful things I said."

"Was Liberty receptive?"

"Yes." He drew on his leather gloves and looked skeptically at the woman, whose age he couldn't fathom due to the strands of gray in her hair yet lack of wrinkles on her face. "Ma'am, if I may inquire of your female expertise, why is it natural to think the person you love will reciprocate your feelings?"

"Would be convenient." She chuckled. "But love never is."

"True."

"You now have a *tondrah* for Liberty, *ja?*"

"No!" At her raised brows, he more calmly answered, "I enjoy being near her but nothing more. She's…different than I remember." *And she captivates me.* Not that he would do anything about his attraction to her.

Where Mrs. Bentz focused, he wasn't sure, but her gaze seemed far away. As if she was thinking of something or maybe someone.

Her husband stopped shoveling the snow. "Ursula," he called out. "Should you need me, across the way I'll be."

With a raised hand, she nodded.

Mr. Bentz grabbed the broom he'd left near an iron lamppost then, with broom in one hand and shovel in the other, crossed the snow-packed street to the two-story white-framed hospital, the slight breeze blowing snow from off the street and nearby unswept rooftops.

He spoke to an elderly couple leaving the hospital. Gerrett recognized them from the train. They'd shared that they were traveling to Chicago to celebrate their fiftieth wedding anniversary. He remembered wondering if fifty years from now would he look upon his bride with such brazen devotion.

He hoped so.

Once the husband tenderly helped his wife down the boardwalk toward the hotel, Mr. Bentz began sweeping the snowdrifts off the wooden planks.

"Mr. Divine," Mrs. Bentz said, smiling slightly as Gerrett looked back to her, "you are a good man."

Gerrett uttered his thanks. He then stepped gingerly backward off the porch. "Might you know the quickest way to the train wreck?"

"*Ja.* The rail tracks parallel main road out of town. About mile you will need to walk to the wreckage." Wrapping her arms around her chest, she brushed her arms as if to warm them. She walked forward. "Follow. We have snowshoes in carriage house."

Gerrett waited until she passed. He then followed her down the shoveled path, snow piled shin-high on either side of the zigzag-patterned walkway.

"Why you need return?" she called over her shoulder. "Sheriff Dawes has a crew of menfolk assisting him, collecting what they can salvage."

"I left my briefcase on the train. It has my house designs, including the floor plans I drew as a proposal gift for Ann."

"Ann?"

"My soon-to-be fiancée."

Mrs. Bentz stopped abruptly, swiveling around, and Gerrett reacted quick enough to prevent bumping into her.

"Fiancée?" she asked, her gaze even with his.

She smelled exactly like Liberty—of home and goodness, of cobblers and fruit, yet the indignation in her expression made him feel all of eight years, instead of his twenty-eight. Here he was a grown man being stared down by a woman five...ten...fifteen years older.

Gerrett shoved his hands in the pockets of his greatcoat. "My parents recently arranged a marriage between myself and a young widow of our acquaintance. I am returning to Chicago to, uhh, officially propose," he said, choking on his own words.

Mrs. Bentz stared at him, her nose and cheeks growing redder in the cold breeze. Then as suddenly as she'd stopped, she turned on her heel and increased her pace to the carriage house. Once inside the cold building, she stepped around a red sleigh. She grabbed a pair of snowshoes from those hanging on the side wall then eased back around the sleigh, still holding the snowshoes to her abundant chest.

"To honor your parents, you will marry Ann, *ja?*"

"Yes, ma'am. She's been a friend of the family for years." Ann was practically a sister to him. With her parents both deceased, his parents had all but adopted her. Ann knew more about his father's business than he did, and with his father's fading eyesight, she'd become his eyes and had legal authority to sign in his name.

Marrying Ann made wise business sense.

"Mr. Divine, ever considered you are doing the right thing for the wrong reason?"

Gerrett released a weary breath. "Numerous times."

She handed him the snowshoes. "That is as foolish as Liberty doing wrong thing for right reason. No wonder you two have connection."

"We don't have a connection."

"Nein?"

"Yes, no connection," Gerrett insisted. "No *tendres.*

I'm not smitten with her, and she no longer feels anything for me."

"My mistake." She smiled then brushed past him to exit the carriage house. "The train wreck is this way, Mr. Divine."

"He needs rescuing, *libelle*."

Despite the frantic increase of her heartbeat, Liberty didn't look up from the potato she was peeling as she stood at the kitchen worktable. She didn't have to ask who Ursula was referring to. Nor would she inquire as to what Ursula and Gerrett discussed during their time outside.

"If you stand closer to the hearth," she said, "you'll warm quicker."

Ursula didn't move from her spot next to Liberty. "A mile trek through snow is too much for one as injured as he."

"Hillsdale's deportment regulations specifically stipulate female students are not to ride with a gentleman without the president's or lady principal's special permission." Liberty shrugged to convey *I have neither.* "I'm sure one of the men in the dining hall can come to Gerrett's aid."

"*Nein,* go you must."

"I think you wish to have me expelled." Curiosity sparked, though, Liberty dropped the potato and knife into the bowl. "Why must I?"

"Because you love him."

No, I obsess over him. Her upper lip curled at how ludicrous that sounded even in her own mind. "He is nothing more to me than my brother's friend."

Ursula made an impatient sound.

Liberty offered a glare that she hoped Ursula would take as an end to the conversation. It wasn't even noon, and she was tired, annoyed and more than mildly cranky. All because she'd minced her heart in a million pieces

then stitched it back together with thread made from de-
luded hope that she'd let her feelings for Gerrett go. Try
as she wanted to, she *truly* hadn't stopped loving him.
Talking to him proved it. And as the tears brimmed in her
eyes, she literally felt the scowl fall from her face into a
brokenhearted chin tremble.

She feared she would always love him.

But someday the hurt would end. Someday her heart
would be healed to love again. Believing that didn't lessen
how awful she felt. Actually, she ached.

She broke Ursula's gaze. "I need to peel—"

"Nein." Ursula pulled the bowl of potatoes out of Liberty's reach. "Leave these to me."

"But—"

"Shh, *mein liebes kind.*" She brushed her knuckles
down Liberty's cheek, sighed, then gripped her shoulders.
"When I was five and twenty, I experienced a magic that
I have spoken of to no one. Until now. I once saw a man
I knew was my other half.

I used to think that about Gerrett.

"His voice, smell and body magnetized me to where I
wanted to be around none but him. Thoughts of him were
on my mind constantly."

I know that, too.

"Until that moment I'd never thought such an experience was truly possible."

Liberty gave Ursula's arm a consoling pat. "You were
blessed to find Josef."

Her voice lowered. "I felt this not for Josef."

Not Josef?

Ursula released Liberty and crossed her hands over her
own heart. She released a ragged breath. "That man did
not love me, but Josef did, and he still wanted to marry
me knowing *tondrah* I had for other man."

"Why did you agree?"

"Marrying Josef vas wise and practical. My friend and my love he's become, and I cannot conceive life without him."

"I can live without—" Ursula shot her a hard look, and Liberty held back the rest of her words.

"Do you feel magnetized to Mr. Divine? Not man in past, but who he is now."

Magnetized? No matter which one of them were the metal and the other the magnet, yes, she felt the captivating pull to him too inconceivable to believe. She wouldn't believe—if she hadn't experienced it herself. It was a horrific and exhilarating feeling. There ought to be an elixir, or at least a two-day sweating sickness, to cure it. Truly, there should.

"I shouldn't, but I do."

"Then go rescue him."

Liberty shook her head.

"Why not?"

"Flee temptation. It's in Scripture."

"Spare him the walk to the collision. What is worse that could happen?"

"I could get expelled riding alone with him."

Ursula's lips pursed tightly. "Expelled for Christian charity?"

Ursula had gone mad. That was the only explanation for this conversation.

"Gerrett doesn't want to see me again."

"You do not know what he wants."

"Maybe," Liberty said tightly.

The Gerrett she'd spoken with wasn't the Gerrett she remembered. That Gerrett would have never admitted his folly or apologized. That Gerrett fled from her presence.

The way this Gerrett looked at her when they shook hands… They'd had a connection. But she couldn't help wonder now if all the fluttering and yearning she felt for him truly was love, or because she was lonely and he was familiar.

She hated not knowing.

Even more so, she hated hoping for something that could never be.

"*Libelle,* what if his feelings for you have changed? I believe he now looks upon you fondly. He's not married, or engaged." When Liberty didn't respond, Ursula added, "Why will you not take a risk for love?"

"I could make an utter fool of myself. Again."

"Or it could turn into something wonderful."

"Or I'd look like a fool," she repeated because Ursula wasn't listening. "Even worse, get expelled."

Ursula shrugged. "Josef has prepared sleigh. Take it and spare Mr. Divine the walk back to town. If not for love, do for Christian charity. Or I will think you are not a nice girl."

"I am a nice girl."

"Then you will go?"

"Only because the poor man is injured and shouldn't be walking in the snow, but—" Liberty sighed. Her heart needed a holiday. "What love I still have for him must stay buried. Even if he were to develop feelings for me—"

"*Ja,* he has."

"—I care for him too much to put him in a situation where my parents would attempt to control him. And they would. Then Gerrett would resent me, as my sister's husband resents her."

Or he'd drown himself like Leonidas's wife had done to escape the trappings and pressure to be perfect and live up to her parents' expectations and demands.

She wouldn't return to that life. Ever. Not even for Gerrett.

"Gerrett Divine is returning to Chicago," she said as

placidly as she could manage, "and I have a life in Hillsdale. Even if he loved me, I will not go back to living in his world."

Chapter 6

When they found him, they'd say, "Now there's one Divine snowman!"

Gerrett stopped walking, drew in a deep, icy breath and released a wry chuckle. Maybe he wasn't *that* frozen or snow-covered, but the back of his trousers were wet from the snow kicking up on him as he'd crossed the wretched packed snow. With the wreck still not within viewing distance, the decision to walk to the collision site seemed even more imprudent amid the snow-capped trees and bright gray sky. A lake was around somewhere. Likely to his left and behind evergreens he knew Miss Judd would cheerfully describe as ethereal.

Miss Judd! *Not* Liberty. He didn't need to think of her by her Christian name.

He didn't need to think of her at all.

What were the statistical chances that the morning after a train collision, he (1) would be walking back to the wreck, (2) in shoes more fitting for the opera than a hike and (3) on snowshoes he expected to fall apart any moment, all because (4) the one woman he never wanted to see again was now the very woman he couldn't get out of his mind?

His mood could not grow any fouler.

"I am not smitten with her," he grumbled to the pine trees. "She is an appealing woman. That's all. I. Am. Going. To. Marry. Ann."

Only Ann didn't have eyes the color of the morning sky as the sun breaks the horizon.

She would never admit that loving anyone made her miserable, as Miss Judd had. She was too controlled to faint over anything. Her presence never made a room warmer to him, but he had given his word that he'd marry Ann. And so he would. Divines always did their duty.

Anger slid like ice down his spine. Why was he so cross? He hadn't felt this antagonism toward his future prior to today, prior to— Liberty's smiling face flashed in his mind. His hand tingled with the memory of the curve of his hand around hers, so soft everywhere except for the calloused tips of her fingers. Gerrett groaned. *This*—whatever it was—was not happening to him.

He needed a moment to reorient his thoughts. And pray.

Spying a downed tree trunk between the road and the railroad tracks, he lifted his right foot, braced for the snow that would smack against his legs and ankles and resumed walking, which was truly more lift right foot and slide left, despite the ache already in his hips. He never liked snowshoeing. Now rowing, skiing, fencing—those were all more agreeable sports. Even croquet. Even ice-skating, especially if it was with Liberty.

Thut, thut, thut went the snow against the back of his trousers, greatcoat and head. Gerrett brushed the snow off his fur collar then drew it closer to his neck. Before he made five steps to the downed trunk, he heard the jingles.

He stopped, looked over his shoulder and felt a burst of joy to the tips of his practically frozen toes.

Liberty drove the sleigh toward him, her hair covered with a blue fur-lined hood.

He grinned.

Something about this new Liberty Adele Judd made him not hate snow so much. He hadn't felt this happy since— He had no idea, but he couldn't stop smiling. While he would eventually return to Chicago and marry Ann, nothing was wrong with enjoying his time with Liberty. She was his closest friend's sister, after all. They'd known each other since she could walk.

He shifted his feet—lift right, slide left—around to face her then waited at the side of the road. Yes, he would say something witty. Or gallant. Or gallantly witty, as a gentleman would to thank the damsel who came to his rescue. That she was riding to liberate him from his wintry trek was certain; how he knew that, he couldn't fathom, nor cared to fathom.

She slowed the sleigh to a stop.

The horse shook his head, his bells jingling.

Her brow furrowed then smoothed again. "Hello."

He nodded his response and waited patiently for her to speak again. Doing so seemed the gentlemanly thing to do when facing a woman who didn't seem as thrilled to see him as he was to see her.

After looping the reins around the hitch, she moved aside the furs covering the seat next to her then, with a gloved hand, patted the wooden bench. "Please."

Gerrett lifted-and-slid-walked forward. He removed the snowshoes and tossed them on the floorboard before easing onto the cold bench next to her.

"Thank you for the rescue."

"You're welcome." She paused. "I need to say something, and I want to get it right, so please give me a moment to steady my nerves."

"Take all the time you need."

Her face tilted. Her eyes so light and unveiled were gazing at him without fear of reprisal, without guile, without any intentional allure to entice him. He admired that about her. Liberty Adele Judd was many things, but a coquette she was not.

He smiled again. He couldn't help it.

The corners of her mouth took on a curve like that of his mother after she had chided him for his misbehavior then said he was her adorable little boy.

Somewhere in the back of his mind, he knew he shouldn't be staring at her lips. Or noting they reminded him of the pink marble he had used in his design of the Marseille château. Nor did he need to notice that the lower one was slightly fuller than the top, and the top one narrower on the edges than in the middle. Not poetic lips. Nor memorable. But intriguing. And wide. The distance apart was the same as the distance between her pupils.

Then they parted, and a rasp of air brushed across them, the sound enough for him to hear.

The last time he had kissed a woman was—

He couldn't remember. Nor could he think of anything save kissing her and how right it would feel. He was cold, she looked warm and she was peering at him with the most remarkable expression, which was why he considered listening—for exactly a fraction of a second—to his conscience advising he ease back on the bench and keep a polite distance between them. But she started speaking and somehow he was removing his gloves and...

"Gerrett," Liberty said with a quaver in her voice, "I need you to—"

He placed his hands on either side of her face and

kissed her. She flinched more so from the frostiness of his touch. Eventually, in hindsight most likely, she would regret not immediately pushing him back, especially since she was sure this violated every jot and tittle of Hillsdale College's deportment rules and regulations. But for seven years, three months and four days, she had dreamed of this moment. Since she was fifteen!

But this—the wonder of his lips growing warm against hers—was more than she'd imagined.

She pulled him closer.

As he kissed her, her old daydreams resurfaced—the beauty and elegance of the wedding service and the ball afterward. Both decorated in lilies and vanilla-scented candles. Dancing and food and their families, and the newspaper reporters writing all that had occurred. Afterward, the operas, balls, soirees, charity fund-raisers, meetings, becoming secretary of the Opera Club and eventual president, gowns and jewels, babies…and loneliness because her father would demand Gerrett put work over family.

Liberty drew back. "No," she said softly between each shatter of her heart. She braced her gloved hand against his chest, keeping distance between them.

He didn't look the least bit disheveled.

He did, however, blink as if he were trying to reconcile what had occurred—more aptly, why *he* kissed *her.* Then came, not to her surprise, the obvious shock that… he had *kissed* her.

Color drained from his face. "Liberty, I can explain."

"Please do."

He ran a hand through his hair, lingering at the back of his neck. "Never mind. I can't."

"I shall presume this was a momentary lapse of judgment." That didn't appear to be what he wanted to hear. "Let us pretend it never happened."

His gaze focused on the floorboard, his breathing sharp. "That would be wise."

Yes, wise. But the kiss had been stupendous, and forgetting her first kiss wasn't something she intended on doing.

After glancing around to ensure no other sleighs or wagons were within viewing distance—and none were—she clenched her hands together in her lap. Good thing she wore gloves or surely her hands would have burned from touching him. Metaphorically speaking, of course.

"I did not save you from your snowy walk for this—" she motioned between them "—to happen."

"I know."

"And you can't hold any blame against me, because I did nothing to entice you to kiss me. I'm not who I used to be."

"I *know!*" Then he muttered, "I'm the fool."

Liberty winced. Whatever reason he had for kissing her clearly wasn't the result of any fond favoring. Having one's love spurned was one thing. Being kissed then rejected was, she supposed, as painful. She pressed her lips together and awkwardly looked around the sleigh. She didn't much like the nausea growing in her stomach as she tried to formulate apt words to ease the tension. Later she'd think of something cordial, clever and considerate. Now all she could come up with was—

"Are you cold?"

"I am quite warm."

His words weren't hostile. They just weren't welcoming.

"You seem agitated."

What he mumbled in French she had no idea, for she was barely passing the class. His eyes closed, his jaw tightened and shifted, and the grinding he was doing to his teeth had to feel unpleasant.

"I'm sorry," she muttered, since apologies, from her experience, tended to soothe tempers.

He grabbed the furs that had fallen to the floorboard and tucked one around her with not the least bit of awareness of how she flinched each time his hands touched her, giving off sparks that she couldn't see yet could intensely feel. Then he cocooned his legs with the second fur and jerked his gloves back on his hands.

He narrowed his eyes at her. "What is it you came here to say?"

"I wasn't completely forthright earlier."

"How so?"

Liberty looked heavenward. Time to swallow the ipecac syrup and rid herself of the poison inside. Figuratively speaking. She had to. For her and, considering he just kissed her, for him, too. Attraction wasn't enough to base a relationship, and she realized that now.

"I watched as society killed my sister's spirit," she said softly. "Like our stepmother, Lurana is now all artifice and pretense. Leonidas drinks because it's one of the few things in his life he can control."

He opened his mouth. "Leo—"

"Please don't defend my brother."

A muscle at his jaw twitched, yet he stayed silent.

"I don't mean to hurt your feelings."

He answered, "You didn't," but what she heard was *I am angry, so finish up what you have to say.*

Liberty twisted her hands in her lap. "I'm attending Hillsdale because I refused to go back into that world again. I would spend my days enduring my parents' attempts to mold me into their image."

"What has that to do with me?"

Growling under her breath, she eased back to put what little additional distance she could between them. "This may not be the most proper thing to admit—" despite wanting to look away, she held his gaze "—but since you kissed me, I know I must say it."

Here's where she was supposed to be forthright, like her family members all were, except her; only forthrightness was easier suggested than done once one was in the exact situation to do it. Clarifying her thoughts with one concise elucidation, her face burned from... She might as well call it mortification. Knowing she'd look like a fool—knowing she'd do something foolish—was why she'd wanted to stay in the kitchen and never see him again.

"Must say what?" he pressed.

Forthrightness was such an overexalted virtue.

"When I am near you," she blurted, "my skin feels awakened."

He didn't draw her to him and ravish her with kisses, and she was glad. Relieved, actually, despite the hurtful ping.

He seemed pensive.

Strangely empowered with courage from confessing her darkest secret, she continued, "Since I was fifteen, your face has been like an image constantly in the back of my mind. Even when I hated you."

He seemed even more pensive.

"When I finally decided to break free of my parents, and everything associated with Chicago society, here you are kissing me."

"Apologizing for the past, that's why I sought you out." He looked away. "The kissing was...unintended." He sounded wretched, which pained her because of all she knew of Gerrett Divine. He had no reason to be sad. Or miserable. Ever.

He had the perfect life. Perfect family. Perfect chin.

She should have felt some empathy for the remorse in his tone. But she hurt down deep where she'd treasured dreams and wasted hours and days and weeks and years thinking of him, of them growing old together. Until death did them part. If she could purge her thoughts and feelings about Gerrett, maybe—*certainly*—then she would be able to return to a world where she was no longer connected to him. Where she was free to not be persnickety in comparing all men to him.

But he had kissed her.

Whether from a momentary lapse of judgment or a growing fondness, he had changed all that was good and well between them. And she allowed him to, because she still hoped for a *someday* with him. Because she wanted to believe that *maybe* his feelings *had* changed toward her.

She gripped the reins, ready to take Gerrett back to Hillsdale.

No. Not yet. No more being a doormat with feelings laid bare for anyone to trample. Even as her heart pounded, she knew this was That Moment Her Life Changed.

"Gerrett, look at me."

His blue eyes met hers, and she didn't look away.

"I want to be desired," Liberty said, growing in confidence. "I want to be pursued. To be chosen. I want to be someone's priority but out of more than momentary lapses of judgment."

Something caught in her throat.

She had wasted years trying to satisfy that yearning with her self-indulgent and embarrassing girlhood fantasy. Wasn't merely Gerrett's love she'd craved. She longed for her father's. But there was no one in this world who could give her the absolute love she needed. She gasped, as the truth of it all sank in. There was no shame in yearning for her father's love, or Gerrett's, or over wanting to be desired and pursued. Or loved. *I am loved, Jesus, and desired and pursued by You.*

Then as bursts of joy fluttered in her heart, filling her with confidence, she smiled.

"Gerrett, I don't *need* you to love me, and I don't *need* to love you." She didn't *need* anyone's love or acceptance or validation but God's, and He'd already given it. Freely. "And that is what I needed to say to you. I forgive you for kissing me, and will not hold your momentary lapse of judgment against you."

She waited again for him to speak.

But he remained silent, looking away from her and swallowing and clearing his throat as if the words in his mouth held an acrimonious taste.

So she said, "I'm sorry for what I said that hurt you."

He nodded.

Liberty adjusted the reins around her hands. "We need to return to the boardinghouse before anyone notices us out here alone. I have no desire to be expelled."

"I can't go back," he finally said, his voice rough. "Not yet."

She turned to face him. She had the odd feeling his *can't go back* referred to more than Hillsdale. "Then where am I taking you?"

"The collision."

"Why?"

"I need to find something important to me."

"You do realize I am not supposed to be riding alone in a sleigh with you?"

"Yes."

Liberty released a resigned breath. She had already broken two deportment rules, not to mention whatever regulation kissing fell under. At this point, what difference would it make? "All right. Since I am risking my collegiate future here at Hillsdale, can you tell me what it is we're going in search of?"

"A gift. For my future fiancée."

Fiancée! She could not speak. She could not think. Surely she had not heard him correctly. Then a voice that sounded like hers said, "Who?"

"Mrs. Ann Bartlett."

Chapter 7

As Liberty drove them to the train wreckage, Gerrett knew he could have been more circumspect in explaining his parental-requested engagement. He could have. He could have omitted any mention of his soon-to-be fiancée and merely cited his missing briefcase and hat, although the latter was of the least concern to him. He certainly could have not shared the name of her older brother's widowed friend. Nor listed ten complimentary traits of Mrs. Ann Bartlett—nine, to be honest, since he was sure he mentioned *mathematical* twice.

There were times when a man shared his inconsiderate thoughts, realized how those inconsiderate thoughts hurt the lady who heard them and then later kicked himself over his own stupidity, before groveling for forgiveness over sharing—over even *thinking*—those inconsiderate thoughts.

This was not one of those times.

Tomorrow he would kick himself.

Even apologize.

At this moment, though, the continued stunned look on Liberty's face brought him deep satisfaction…and a little guilt…not to mention a heap of shame, although he was quite content to ignore the latter two emotions.

Ignoring emotions was one of the privileges of being a man.

I forgive you for kissing me—

She had shot a bullet through the last modicum of his pride.

—and will not hold your momentary lapse of judgment against you.

And he wasn't quite ready to let that go. He was angry. Her sharing in his pain—it wasn't heroic of him to admit—brought him a bit of juvenile gratification to atone for his shattered pride.

He shouldn't have kissed Liberty. Hadn't intended to. But an inexplicable thread drew him to her. In the basest explanation of all—he desired her. He couldn't *not* kiss her. As a gentleman, as a man returning home to propose to another woman, he should feel guilty. He should. His conscience screamed at him. Yet he felt not an ounce of guilt.

Not only had he enjoyed kissing her, he wanted to do it again.

And he wanted her to want him to kiss her again, not forgive him for it, which only made him angrier.

"We're here," Liberty said.

Gerrett straightened in the seat and looked at the sight before him. Although the fires were out, ashes from the burned eastbound mail car fluttered in the breeze, giving it a pungent smell. His best guess, the cleanup and repair would take a week. But whether on horse or with buggy or sleigh, somehow he would make it to Chicago.

Ann will make a superb wife, superb wife, superb wife,

he thought, resuming the chant he'd begun after boarding the ship in Le Havre, France.

His duty, as the Divine heir, was to marry Ann Bartlett.

"Makes good business sense," he muttered.

"What was that?"

"Nothing of consequence."

"I believe if one has something to say, one shouldn't mutter it."

"For men, muttering is an acceptable form of conversation."

Liberty stopped the sleigh near the westbound wreckage where several other horses and wagons stood. Voices called out from those unloading the baggage cars to those loading the wagons.

She tied the leads down. "I'll help you look."

"No, stay." He took the fur blanket from his lap and wrapped it around her lap and shoulders. "It's safer. I'll be back in a moment, and then we can return to Hillsdale and you can be done with me."

Her eyes watered up from the cold; he wasn't going to think it was from any other reason. Anger, right now, was the safest emotion for him to feel.

"Gerrett, I'm sorry for what I said that hurt—"

"Don't. Please." His pride couldn't endure another apology.

He reclaimed the snowshoes from the backseat of the sleigh, tied them to his feet, then began the lift-slide march—*thut, thut, thut* went the snow against his back—to the passenger car that held the last bit of Gerrett Divine, architect.

Liberty drew the fur up to her chin as she watched Gerrett talk to Sheriff Dawes and the other men wedging boards under the fallen passenger car while others attached a pair of oxen to the other side. To lift it? They could be here for who knows how long if they had to wait on the passenger car to be set back on its wheels, instead of allowing Gerrett to climb inside and look for his treasured engagement gift. For his fiancée. For—

Ann Bartlett?

Tension burrowed in her forehead.

Of all the women to marry, he had to choose one of the few ladies in society whom she actually liked and could be close friends with *if* she lived in Chicago. During the past five years Gerrett had been in France, Ann Hershberger Bartlett had dutifully married an aged man her parents had chosen, miscarried four times, lost a baby at birth and became a widow by age twenty-seven. Ann could quote the entire book of James.

Why *wouldn't* Gerrett's parents and grandparents believe she would be a suitable wife for the Divine heir? Everyone in Chicago society—probably all of the ninety-thousand people in Chicago—loved Ann.

Two months ago at the Opera Club's annual Christmas Ball, she'd thanked Ann for being Leonidas's lone friend whose faith was more than Sunday-morning rituals. Not only did Ann defend Leonidas when others blamed him for his wife's suicide, she grieved her spiteful husband's death and then, to society's chagrin, donated most of his wealth to religious charities and missions. If any woman deserved a man who desired, pursued and prioritized her, that was Ann Hershberger Bartlett.

Liberty adored Ann. And Gerrett Divine was going to marry her.

Yet he kissed me, *knowing full well the kindhearted woman awaiting his proposal. The oaf!* Liberty kicked the footboard of the sleigh for good measure. Ann deserved someone better than Gerrett. Even with his perfect chin.

Thinking how she was risking expulsion being seen alone with him in a sleigh, she slumped on the bench. For

Ann's sake, she rather he had married some French heiress who ate snails. If she hadn't already shared enough
of today, she would tell him exactly what she thought of
his ungentlemanly behavior.

A gift for his fiancée?

She released a "pffft." It was probably a piece of jewelry, the typical engagement gift. Diamonds. Maybe
pearls. She took smug pleasure in knowing Ann Bartlett
cared not one iota for fancy rings and pretty necklaces.

Once Gerrett found what he lost in the collision, she
would return him to Hillsdale and be done with him, all
right. The sooner he was gone, the sooner she'd also stop
feeling sorry for hurting him.

Her gaze settled on Gerrett climbing atop the railcar.
He stood and wobbled. Her breath caught. *Jesus, keep
him safe.*

Gerrett dropped down into the passenger car and stared
at the devastation. Papers, clothes, books and other per-
sonal items littered what was now the floor of the car.
After he'd helped everyone exit the railcar, someone had
climbed inside and searched through the bags and por-
table valets.

"Someone's been in here," he called out to Sheriff
Dawes.

"We know," came the weary voice back. "Get what you
need, Mr. Divine. We need to get this car upright. Mayor
Parker has a list started of what's missing."

Gerrett drew in a deep breath. Inside his leather briefcase had been a pearl necklace he'd bought from a jew-
eler in Le Havre, despite knowing Ann cared little for
opulent gifts. Still, it seemed a more fitting engagement
gift than house designs alone. The money and jewelry he
expected to be stolen. The drawings had to be there, all

neatly rolled, bound with leather and tied with a yellow satin ribbon. Had to.

Yet with seeing everything tossed about, his stomach tensed. The number of days he'd spent planning, then drawing and redrawing—he didn't want to think about it.

The designs were almost irreplaceable.

No sense dawdling. He stepped on the wood and window frames, taking care not to break any additional glass, determined to reach the bench where he'd sat. His heart pounded frantically in his chest to where he could have sworn he saw his shirt moving. *It'll be there. It will.*

Lying near the window was his gray felt derby.

It'll be there.

"It will," he muttered.

Gerrett eased closer. Scooping up his hat, he turned, fought to steady his heartbeat and looked down.

"Miss Judd, I am done here."

Liberty stopped praying, opened her eyes and looked to Gerrett sliding onto the sleigh bench. His mere presence set her heart to pounding. As he sat the brown leather briefcase and gray hat in the space between them, he didn't look happy.

"Did you find—"

"No."

She wanted to tell him she was sorry for his loss. That she understood his having spent time to search for the perfect gift and sympathized with his grief over not finding it. Mostly, that Ann Bartlett would have treasured it, because Ann was that type of a lady. But her compassion for him and vexation with him were causing an emotional stew of confusion.

She handed him the spare fur. "Here."

He wrapped it around his legs.

Liberty untied the reins then flicked them. Within minutes, they left the train wreckage behind. On the trip back, the sleigh seemed to find every rock or bump in the road.

"Gerrett, I—"

"Silence is comforting," he said stiffly.

Liberty nodded, although she didn't know why. The silence comforted her not in the least.

In the silence, she became aware how every hair on her neck seemed to stand at knowing how close they sat even with a briefcase between them, how loud her heart was beating, how much she wished to ease close and share his warmth.

Liberty gripped the reins tighter around her gloves.

As the sleigh glided and occasionally bumped across the packed snow, she glanced down at the briefcase then slowly raised her gaze to see he was watching her. He stared unblinking, long enough for her to give him her best I-am-sorry-for-your-loss expression. *Zing* went her heart. And she was fine with it because someday soon her uncontrollable internal responses to him would come to an end.

When he didn't look away, she offered a smile, a soft upturn to the right corner of her mouth. Then, because it seemed the right thing to do, she handed him the reins. He nodded ever so slightly and took control of the sleigh.

When they passed the side road leading to the Freed estate, he broke the silence.

"The house designs I drew were stolen."

"Were they your gift for Ann?"

"Yes. I also bought her a pearl necklace."

"Ann would have loved it," she answered, trying to sound casual instead of elated at finally being able to speak.

He slowed the sleigh as they approached the village's outer limits. "No, she wouldn't have."

True, but no need to compliment him for knowing his

future fiancée that well. She hadn't quite worked out that bit of jealousy. "Perhaps the mercantile has a suitable replacement."

"One simply does not go to the mercantile to purchase a gift for the woman one is proposing to."

Liberty pinched her lips closed to halt an immediate and snappish response. His foul mood she could excuse considering the engagement gift he'd purchased had been stolen. But the condescension in his tone was intolerable.

"The Gerrett Henry Divine I met this morning in the boardinghouse kitchen would have never said anything so high-nosed."

He didn't move.

He didn't speak.

He gave no indication her words affected him.

"My friend Charlie gave his wife a thimble as an engagement gift," she continued. "A thimble! I watched him in the mercantile for an hour as he agonized over buying the perfect one to show his devotion."

He still didn't speak.

"She carries it in a satchel she wears around her neck every day. It's nothing impressive, yet she treasures it."

"I'm not giving my fiancée a thimble."

He said *thimble* with such disdain that she momentarily lost all thoughts of a response.

She counted to ten then sweetly said—

"You are a prig."

He glared at her.

She glared back, albeit with somewhat of a smirk, because for some inexplicable reason, saying those words made her feel rather proud of herself. The former Doormat Liberty would have never been so candid.

Another jingle-bell-bedecked sleigh approaching on the left slowed, the driver frantically waving as he passed the outskirts of Hillsdale.

Liberty lost her smirk. John Emery? What could he want?

"Stop the sleigh," she ordered.

Gerrett obeyed.

She waved at the burly coppersmith as their sleighs halted to where they were side by side. His face, what she could see above his beard, was flushed.

"Good morning, Mr. Emery. Is something wrong?"

"Wrong?" He practically bounced on his seat, which made the bells on his sleigh jingle. "No, Miss Judd, everything is right as rain. Got a telegram this morn. Miss Uptograss has consented to be my wife."

Much could be said for persistence, considering the man had proposed to Miss Mary Uptograss of Osseo well before Liberty had moved to Hillsdale. "Congratulations! When is the wedding?"

Gerrett must have tugged on the reins because their horse shook his head, causing his bells to jingle and the sleigh to shift then stop.

Mr. Emery leaned back on his bench as if to get a better perspective for seeing who sat next to her in the sleigh. His gaze settled on Gerrett, morphed into a disapproving scowl, then with renewed cheer in his light brown eyes moved back on her. "That's what I needed to speak to you about. I ripped the other sleeve of my Sunday suit."

Liberty nodded her understanding. This would make the fifth alteration this year for Mr. Emery and his poorly sewn suit. "How soon do you need it?"

"How soon?" Mr. Emery tugged on the ragged edge of his beard. "Uhh, you see," he said sheepishly, his cheeks brightening, "the Reverend Burton said he'd perform the vows as soon as I can bring Miss Uptograss to Hillsdale."

She chuckled. "Immediately then. I'll work on it after I take Mr. Divine to the depot to see when the next stage is running."

"It don't run during winter months. Train passengers are stranded here until the train gets running again."

Liberty touched Gerrett's arm. "I can see if the Bentzes have a spare room in the boardinghouse, unless you wish to stay at the hotel."

"Uhh, well now," Mr. Emery stuttered.

"That would be perfect, *cherie*." He grinned, a devilish curve to his lip that, were she made of weaker stuff, would have made her sigh. Instead, her heart skipped a beat, some internal butterflies danced and—

She blinked and jerked her hand from his arm. She was past this.

"Mr. Divine," she blurted, "you mistake my—"

"Congratulations on the wedding, Mr. Emery," Gerrett said. "Miss Uptograss is a lucky woman."

Mr. Emery's brow furrowed like it did when she knew he was at the boardinghouse and overheard the Quackenbush twins discussing a new algebraic equation. He was thinking hard to make sense of something. Likely, if he was supposed to be offended, or complimented, by Gerrett's words.

He scratched his forehead. "Miss Judd, should you be riding alone—"

"It's fine," she rushed out with an oh-don't-pay-it-no-mind wave of her hand. "Principal Whipple is… Ehrm, she and I talk. Of things. The weather. My grade in natural theology. Courting." Well, not really courting. "Mr. Emery, about that coat of yours…"

"I left it with Mrs. Bentz. She said you were out this way," he added. "Didn't say you had someone with you."

"Mr. Divine is *merely* an old family friend." Liberty tossed her best smile at the coppersmith. "Shouldn't you be getting on to Osseo?"

"Osseo?" Mr. Emery repeated.

"To Miss Mary Uptograss," she clarified.

He nodded, somewhat shamefaced. After one final scowl in Gerrett's direction, Mr. Emery and his sleigh headed off down the road to Osseo.

"Merely?" Gerrett groused.

"Would you rather have preferred I put the emphasis on *old?* Or, even better, *friend?*"

Instead of coming up with a smashing retort or even an excusable mutter, he flicked the reins and started their horse-drawn sleigh into motion.

Liberty shifted on the seat, sliding her right leg onto the bench and tucking it and her crinoline under her as she turned to face him. *"Cherie?"* she said, readjusting the fur covering her skirts. "Care to explain that endearment?"

"It's what men do."

"It's what men do?"

"Yes."

"Men are illogical."

"Yes, we are." He turned his head a fraction, just enough for their gazes to meet. "Even more so when a comely lady is in attendance."

"Are you implying Mr. Emery favors me?"

"You can't see it?"

"He is affianced."

"Sometimes a man has no choice but to settle for second best."

"A compliment to be sure." She tried to keep her voice even as she struggled between being amused by or annoyed with him. "And yet I cannot help but feel offense on Miss Uptograss's and Ann Bartlett's behalf."

Gerrett stopped the sleigh at the village's first intersection. He hadn't intended his words to denigrate either lady, yet they had. He, thankfully, had enough sense not to dig himself a deeper hole as common to those of his gender.

"My apologies. Both ladies will make superb wives."

Gerrett looked down both side streets. He should remember the direction to the Bentzes' boardinghouse, but now wagons, sleighs and pedestrian traffic on the snow-packed streets lessened his ability to recall from where he'd started walking. Something roasting in the nearby café added to his distraction and prompted a stomach growl.

"Which way to the boardinghouse?"

Liberty was looking him over. Her eyes intent on his, searching, he suspected, for truth of the sincerity of his earlier words or anything to give proof otherwise.

Someone called her name.

She glanced away long enough to wave at a male and female group of what looked to be college students from the numerous books they carried. Hillsdale was her village—the place where he suspected everyone knew her. Anything she did, anyone she courted, would be fodder for all to know.

When she looked back at him, her gaze held compassion and curiosity. "Gerrett, why did you agree to an arranged marriage with Ann?"

"Marrying Ann makes practical business sense. I need a wife to provide me an heir, and she knows Father's business enough to help me learn it." While gripping the reins in his right hand, he drew his fingers down to the reins' ends. "Boardinghouse directions?"

"Morning!" Miss Olive Wittingham called out as she drew up to the sleigh on Gerrett's side. She held hands with the boy Samuel, who appeared too enchanted with the redhead to notice anyone else.

Liberty waved again. "Morning, Olive! I have your gown repaired."

Miss Wittingham's gaze shifted to Gerrett, and although she looked at him questioningly, she acknowledged him with only a nod. "I'll pick my dress up later, if that's all right."

"Certainly."

Miss Wittingham and Samuel continued down the street.

Liberty shifted on the bench to face forward. "Ann Bartlett will make an exceptional wife."

Gerrett nodded because his mind and heart knew that, yet he couldn't conjure a smidgen of desire toward marrying Ann. "Directions?"

"Two streets up then turn left, please."

They rode in silence to the boardinghouse, which was fine with Gerrett. Whether or not Liberty agreed with his reasons for marrying Ann, he accepted that his life was no longer his own.

Chapter 8

As they pulled into the boardinghouse's drive, Josef Bentz waited for them to stop at the carriage house. He helped Liberty out of the sleigh and onto the bricked walk, like the doting father she had before her mother died.

Gerrett grabbed his briefcase and hat—such high quality she was surprised it hadn't been stolen, too—and followed her down the path, surrounded on each side by shin-high piles of snow. Something nagged at her. Something he'd said earlier lingered in the back of her mind. Something about—

She stopped on the third step leading up to the boardinghouse's front porch and swirled around. "*You* drew designs for a house?"

"I am an architect." His grip tightened on his hat and briefcase. "I trained in France."

"Then why do you need Ann to help you learn your father's business?"

"He's dying."

"I'm so sorry."

"When the disease began to weaken his eyesight, Ann volunteered to read all documents for him. For all practical purposes, she is his eyes. She knows more about his investments and accounting than anyone."

"Ann enjoys math."

"Yes, she does." Gerrett tapped the hat against his thigh; his eyes were sad. "I've been sketching the design since I was a teen. I intended them to be an engagement gift someday. Replacing the pearl necklace matters not to me. Those drawings…" He didn't have to continue for her to understand the significance of his loss.

A pearl necklace would never win Ann's affection.

But architectural drawings of a house?

When Ann first married Mr. Bartlett, Liberty swore it was because Ann had fallen in love with Mr. Bartlett's lakeside estate, because why else marry a man three times her age? Selling it later hadn't been by desire, Ann had shared, but a practical decision. What did a childless widow need with a three-story, eighteen-room house surrounded by the most beautiful gardens in Illinois? A suite in the Tremont House now provided Ann living space but was "too impersonal and confined" to ever be a home to her—the only complaint she'd *ever* heard Ann make.

Could there be a more romantic gift?

Dizzy, Liberty grabbed the wooden handrail next to the steps. Oh, she felt sick. Clearly, she still hadn't worked out that last—large—bit of jealousy.

"Liberty?" he said, his tone and eyes full with concern.

She swallowed again, trying to work up her nerve to ask what she needed to hear. "Gerrett, did you draw those plans with Ann in mind?"

"Not specifically her," he rushed out, and she wanted to imagine that she heard mortification in his tone. "I knew

I would marry someday. Giving them to her is fitting—was fitting. They're gone now."

Fitting? Good gracious, they were more than fitting. They would have made the ideal engagement gift, and there was no reason why he couldn't recreate them. She had lost her mind. Why would she do anything to help Gerrett propose to another woman?

Love one another.

Be kind to one another.

Do unto others as you would have done unto you.

Surely there was a Scripture verse that said, "Liberty, be selfish and don't help Ann's chance for a marriage where she will be loved and treasured." Yet the only one surfacing in her consciousness was one she'd read upon rising this morning: *Let your conduct be without covetousness.* Another reminder that God knew the verses she needed each day.

How easy would it be to run inside with nothing more than a fare-thee-well! Her cheeks were cold. Her lips were cold. But the right thing to do was to help him. Maybe giving selflessly was what her heart needed to do to heal. Yes, that was it! She would be his friend and aid him with his proposal. She wanted him to be happy and she wanted Ann to be happy, even if that meant their being happy together.

She released a weary, self-focused breath.

There in the rich depths of her heart grew hope, budding with the knowledge that once Gerrett left Hillsdale and established his future in Chicago, she would love again. She'd make sure of it. And she'd help herself, starting this very moment, by helping him.

"You are going to redraw those designs," she ordered.

He shook his head. "I don't have enough time."

"The railroad has track to repair, snow to clear off and

wreckage to clean up. Whether you wish it or not, you are stranded here all weekend and likely through next week."

"I could buy a horse and start out for Chicago on my own."

"You could." She grinned. "But no lady wishes to be proposed to by a man with a bruised, egg-size knot on his temple, no matter how handsome he is."

He rested the heel of his shoe on the boardinghouse's first step, his elbow on the stair rail. "My dear Miss Judd, one simply does not go to the mercantile to buy sheets of vellum. Practically, not priggishly, speaking." His blue eyes twinkled with merriment. Like a friend would share with another when they were in on a secret laugh.

"True, Mr. Divine, one simply does not buy sheets of vellum at a mercantile, but I know where we could find something you can use."

"Where?"

The moment she said, "Hillsdale College," Gerrett thought her idea might be possible. He had the rest of the supplies he needed. His T-square, set squares, rulers, protractor, compasses, pencils and drawing pens were all securely locked in his luggage, which Sheriff Dawes and the railroad employees were loading in wagons to be brought to Hillsdale later in the day.

In seven days he could redraw a site plan and a house floor plan. If he could focus without distraction, working from sunup to past sundown, he could have a front elevation drawn, too. A simple sketch, of course. Later, he could embellish his drawings.

Gerrett stared absently at the boardinghouse door behind Liberty.

As he'd spent years drawing and redrawing until he'd perfected the design, all he had to do was close his eyes and the images were clear in his mind. The facade. The axes. The cutting of the vertical plane. He used to think his ability to see and draw dimensional shapes where others only saw and drew flat objects was a curse. Until he discovered architecture.

He looked to Liberty.

She was watching him intently. There in her blue-gray eyes, though, was something he hadn't seen since he walked into the boardinghouse kitchen earlier: excitement. Like she was about to start a new adventure and was beseeching him to join in. And he would.

He would draw Liberty a house—correction, he would draw a house because she wanted him to and because he wanted to, and…because he felt hopeful. Someday he would look back on this exuberant, painful, confusing train wreck of a collision with Liberty Judd and acknowledge God really did weave the joys *and* hardships of life into something beautiful. He didn't know what the future held, but he knew everything would work out right. For both of them. Even for Ann.

In the meantime, he could enjoy being friends with Liberty.

"Before we begin this 'Quest to Find Vellum for Gerrett,'" he said, grinning, "might I impose upon you for a meal?" His stomach chose that moment to echo his request.

Liberty chuckled. "Follow me."

After a quick stop at the telegraph office for him to notify his family of the wreck, his safety and the delay home, Gerrett walked with Liberty to the Hillsdale College campus. He told her about the château he'd designed, his first project after finishing his training. They carefully climbed the snow-cleared steps leading to the bricked four-story building's front entrance.

Gerrett held the door open for Liberty. She stepped inside, and he followed.

"Afternoon." A dark-haired gentleman tipped his top hat as Gerrett closed the door. He was older than Gerrett by only a few years, and had deep, chiseled cheeks. "Timely visit, Miss Judd."

"Oh?" she answered cheerfully, but Gerrett heard the underlying alarm. Her gaze shifted to the dozen or so college students milling about the front foyer; others were sitting in chairs and settees and talking, many, though, looking at them. "I heard classes were canceled for the day."

"They were. I was leaving to find you."

"Sir, I know my grade on the last Latin exam isn't to your satisfaction, but do know it is a poor reflection of me, the student, not you, the gracious tutor, nor Lady Principal Whipple, the ever diligent and dedicated professor."

"Your test grade we can discuss another time. And we will." A wrinkle between his eyebrows deepened, yet a small muscle ticked along his jawline as if fighting a laugh. His voice lowered to where only they could hear. "Word has it you and a gentleman were riding in a sleigh unchaperoned, and neither I nor Miss Whipple recall giving special permission."

Liberty looked entirely panicked. "I'm sorry, sir. I, uhh—"

"She was with me," Gerrett offered without shame. He shrugged off his heavy greatcoat and draped it over his left arm. "In Christian charity, Miss Judd rescued me from a snowy walk to the wreck site. My toes offer her their undying gratitude."

"I see." The man's gaze shifted between Liberty and Gerrett.

"President Fairfield—" she touched Gerrett's forearm "—this is Mr. Gerrett Divine, an old family friend returning home to Chicago. The train wreck stranded him. Mr. Divine, this is the esteemed Edmund Burke Fairfield, president of the college."

Of all the aspirations Gerrett had, being a president of a college by his thirties was not one of them. Owning the premier architectural firm in Chicago...

They shook hands and exchanged nice-to-meet-yous.

"Mr. Divine is an architect." Liberty pulled the gloves off her hands, and Gerrett helped her remove her hooded cloak. "Thank you," she whispered over her shoulder to him, and he felt her warm breath raise the hairs on the backs of his hands.

He stood there frozen, transfixed, searching for an explanation for his response to what he knew to be an action she never intended to be alluring.

"He trained in Paris," Liberty said, drawing Gerrett's attention back to the moment.

Fairfield's heavy brows rose. "You don't say."

"Académie des Beaux-Arts." Thankful for a conversation to distract him from the thread he felt pulling him to Liberty, Gerrett draped her cloak over his greatcoat. "I don't know if you're familiar—"

"Quite familiar," Fairfield interjected, his expression warming even more. "It is the foremost school for music, architecture, painting and sculpture in all of Europe. My wife's second cousin applied three times to the academy of music and ended up attending a school in England, instead. Your talent must be great."

Gerrett glanced at Liberty. She was regarding him quizzically. He probably should have explained earlier where he had received his training.

"What talent I have comes from God and years of practice," he said humbly. Though his maternal second cousin, Jean-Baptiste Lesueur, was a member of the Académie. Being related had earned him an honest consideration. His skill earned him placement. After noting the number of male students watching them from the seating area behind Liberty, he eyed the dark woodwork framing the walls and vaulted ceiling. "This is a fine building you have."

Fairfield nodded. "Yes, but we are often criticized that the architecture is plainer than most schools have."

"I think our dome is pretty." Liberty then grimaced as if she felt a fool for speaking up.

Gerrett smiled, touching her wrist. "The dome is pretty. And symmetrical." Realizing the degree to which he wanted to hold her hand and stake his claim in front of all the men in the room watching Liberty, he drew back. "According to Roman architect Vitruvius, a good building should satisfy the three principles of *firmitas, utilitas, venustas.*"

Fairfield gave a little nod of his head at Liberty, as if to say, *Translate, please.*

"Durability, utility and beauty."

"Excellent! That earns you five extra credit points on your test."

"Considering how *egnus* I am for those points," Liberty said, smiling, "then I shall not begrudge the *simplicitas* of the question. Perhaps five more credit points for Latin usage in everyday speech?"

"Duly noted, Miss Judd." Fairfield grinned. "Duly noted."

"Using those criteria," Gerrett could not help commenting, "this building, no matter how plain anyone defines her to be, satisfies those principles. Standing on the highest grounds in the area, she presents an imposing appearance. A lady worthy of praise."

"Divine, should you consider a life molding the minds of young architects, we have a place for you here at Hillsdale." Fairfield focused on Gerrett. "A pleasure to meet you. We are having a Saint Valentine's Day Social next week. You're welcome to attend if you are still in town, and if you need anything during your stay in Hillsdale, let me know."

"You wouldn't by chance know if there is any unused vellum on campus?" Gerrett asked.

"No, but, Miss Judd, would you see Mr. Divine to the museum? Goswell is in there playing with the weapons again.... I mean, working on his history notes. If there is vellum here, he will know. Do remember, our deportment rules are for your protection."

"Yes, sir." She lowered her voice. "Thank you for not expelling me."

He softly answered, "Consider this your first warning."

Fairfield, who was clearly trying to restrain his own laughter, placed his top hat on his head. "Now that I have attended to the quandary named Miss Judd, I shall enjoy the remainder of this wintry day with my wife. Good day to you both."

Fairfield headed to the front doors then outside, letting in a burst of cold air that made the hem of Liberty's paisley skirt flutter. The door closed.

With pursed lips, Liberty looked at the group of students.

To Gerrett's surprise, she cheerfully announced for all to hear, "Everyone, this is Gerrett Divine of late from France. He is an old family friend, journeying home to Chicago. Due to the train collision, he is temporarily stranded in our village, so please make him feel welcome. Gentlemen, he is no threat. Ladies, he is taken."

"What about you, Miss Judd?" someone called out. "Are you taken?"

Chapter 9

Gerrett was too stunned by the question to come to Liberty's defense before Liberty whirled around to face a man standing near the west fireplace.

"Fred Quackenbush, *that* is an improper question."

"He's George. I'm Fred," said the identical-looking man sitting on a settee, who seemed more interested in the book he was reading than anything else.

The man at the fireplace shrugged.

"I...uhh," Liberty sputtered, her cheeks red.

Gerrett stepped forward, blocking Liberty from the man's view. "Mr. Quackenbush, I believe the Saint Valentine's Day Social would be the perfect opportunity for you and Miss Judd to discuss her takenness—or lack thereof. Perhaps over a scone and lemonade?"

After all, times like this called for diplomacy and decorum. And Mr. Quackenbush seemed a reasonable fellow, which was why Gerrett would accompany Liberty to the social…and ensure the man had no opportunity to woo, bring lemonade to or even gaze wistfully upon her.

"Miss Judd," Gerrett asked, "is that reasonable?"

The left side of her upper lip curled a fraction, yet she said, "Certainly."

Quackenbush's eyes narrowed. He finally nodded, and the students in the foyer lost their interest in Gerrett and Liberty and resumed socializing with one another.

Gerrett smiled at Liberty. "You certainly know how to introduce a gentleman."

"Forthrightness is a virtue—" her face took on a lofty expression "—something I need to develop more in my life."

"Says who?"

She looked at him as if the question was ridiculous. "Me," she said in an obliging tone. "Compared to everyone in my family, I am too cautious, reticent and guarded, which only empowers them to think they have the authority to dictate my thoughts and actions."

Her, reticent? He couldn't imagine this new Liberty sitting idly aside while anyone tried to force her to do or think what she didn't want to. A cautious young woman would not leave all she knew and attend college in another state, hundreds of miles from home. A guarded woman would not admit to a man that her skin felt awakened when he was near.

The words slipped softly from his lips. "You are more than you think you are."

There was a slight pause, and he knew she didn't know what to respond. Then she said, "Follow me."

As they walked, a group of fellow students looked their way but said nothing more than "Welcome to Hillsdale." Gerrett nodded his response to them. He wasn't sure where Liberty was headed, still he followed.

"I did not realize you were an artist," she said.

"I'm not an artist. I see buildings in my mind and can draw all aspects and dimensions of them." He glanced sideways at her as they walked at a nonbrisk pace. "Were I to do a portrait of the loveliest girl I know, she would turn into Quasimodo, but ask me to draw the Notre-Dame Cathedral, and I can."

The corner of her mouth indented.

They placed their outer garments in the cloakroom then headed across the marble floor toward the western portion of the building. They passed more students. How many had he overheard were enrolled? Upward of one hundred and fifty, at least half of whom were presently on the first floor of the building.

When she said no more, he asked, "Are you taking scientific courses or the classics?"

"Scientific?" She shuddered. "Only those I must."

"Then which of the classics do you favor? Latin? French? Philosophy? History? Theology?"

She shuddered again, this time with an unladylike "Blah."

Gerrett couldn't restrain his laughter. "If you don't enjoy studies, Liberty, then why attend college?"

"To escape."

"From?"

"The expectations my parents have of me." Slowing their pace, she turned her head and gazed at him frankly. "I love my parents, but I do not wish to be around them."

Her brother had confessed the very same thing last month in Marseille. "What life would you prefer, instead?"

She focused forward. "A simple one. Here in the township of Hillsdale, with a husband and children and my sewing."

"Don't let Quackenbush hear you, or he will carry you off to the Reverend Scott for a wedding."

This time she laughed, and the musical sound echoed in the corridor. "I doubt the good reverend will want to perform *those* vows."

Now that had him curious. In light of Burton Scott's unwillingness to share Liberty's name, Gerrett had to ask, "Is he another conquest?"

She let out an unladylike snort.

Gerrett did a quick about-face, walking backward so he could watch the play of emotions in her expression. "Miss Judd, exactly how many men in this village have *tendres* for you?"

"I am not attending Hillsdale to earn a marriage degree."

"You didn't answer my question."

"And you should conclude something from that." She smiled as if she were pleased with her answer.

Gerrett was about to make a smashing retort, but then Liberty knocked him speechless with—

"Leonidas said last summer you were engaged to a French heiress, the daughter of an aristocrat."

He blinked.

"Who eats snails and caviar," she added.

He blinked again.

"And drinks wine from a shoe."

That made him laugh. "Drinks wine from a shoe?"

She shrugged. "Seems the French thing to do."

He opened his mouth, but no sounds came out.

She waved off her words as if they were an annoying fly. "Pay me no mind. I'm sure I read the latter in a novel, and one cannot believe everything she reads. Especially about French heiresses." He almost thought she was being serious until he saw the tightening of her lips as if she were trying to maintain a straight face.

"I turned her down," he admitted dryly.

She halted and grabbed the front of his waistcoat, stopping him. "A wealthy French aristocrat who eats snails and caviar and drinks wine from her shoes actually proposed? To you?"

After their kiss, he couldn't have imagined having a conversation like this. Doing it now felt…right. He wanted to be her friend. He wanted to laugh and joke and confess secrets. And he wished he had the artistic skill to capture on canvas the way her wide, unpoetic lips curved ever so slightly, ever so invitingly.

Realizing where he was staring, he looked away and cleared his throat. One didn't kiss one's friends.

"Yes, she proposed, although her wine-in-shoe drinking is pure literary fabrication."

Liberty gave an I-cannot-believe-the-boldness-of-some-women shake of her head. "My decision to enroll in Hillsdale was instigated after a humiliating proposal from one of my father's lawyers."

"Your parents willingly allowed you to attend college?"

"Father and I negotiated an agreement. He allows me to take classes for two semesters. In June I return home and choose between two suitors."

Every muscle in his body tensed. Teasing her about her conquests was one thing. Knowing she was to marry and had willfully agreed to it— Not even the blandest of congratulations would pass his lips. He couldn't let her do this.

He couldn't let her ruin her life.

"Who are the suitors?" he managed to ask graciously, instead of grabbing her arms and demanding to know why she had agreed to such foolishness. But by the look in her eyes, he knew she wouldn't give him the names even if he offered to the last penny of his inheritance. "Why did you make the agreement?"

Her gaze fell to where she still gripped his waistcoat.

Gerrett held his breath. The need to know twisted his gut.

"No one says no to my father," she said softly.

Liberty spoke the truth. Gerrett held silent, unable to find a kind word to say about Edward Judd.

She released her hold then looked around the hallway. "On Wednesday," she whispered, even though the nearest people were at the other end of the hall, "my parents received a letter from the Reverend Scott, asking for permission to court me. They panicked, thinking I would marry someone not..." She grimaced.

"Not suitable to their standards?" he supplied.

She nodded. "Last night before my stepmother's birthday ball, Father told me I couldn't return to Hillsdale and that I had to accept his associate's marriage proposal. I fled, and I am never returning to Chicago. I don't owe them my future, and they have no right to it."

Gerrett winced. As the last of the Divines, his duty was to marry and produce sons to carry on the name. Most of his life so far had been spent thinking and living for himself. Even though his father and grandfather still lived, he was, if not the head of the family, the future. He had a duty to them, and he was going to honor it.

Even though it meant letting go of his heart's desire, taking over the family business and marrying Ann.

Leaving Gerrett to ponder her words, Liberty stepped to the museum's opened door and glanced inside. True to President Fairfield's word, Ayden Goswell stood inside, gripping the two-handed hilt of a long sword in his left hand, a pencil in the other hand as he wrote notes in his journal that sat on a display case. His hair was darker than Gerrett's, about the same length, though not as untamed on top, and she did not wish in that moment to debate the fine merits of a man having coiffed, oiled, long, short or untamable hair.

A tingle inched up her spine. She didn't have to look to know Gerrett now stood behind her.

Instead, she kept her thoughts on the man holding the medieval weapon. The inches Professor Goswell had on Gerrett in height, Gerrett made up in the breadth of his shoulders. Like many of her female classmates who openly admitted their admiration of Ayden Goswell, she'd concluded that her history professor would make a fine husband.

If he weren't so scholarly bent.

An engagement gift from him would probably be a gold-embossed copy of *Don Quixote* and some antique gem his mother would have to remind him repeatedly to purchase. Still, he was an excellent professor and man of character, so she continued to pray the college would hire him to permanently fill the vacancy he was temporarily filling.

"Professor?" she said, stepping onto the wooden floor.

He looked up, and as his blue-eyed gaze settled on her, he smiled. "Ahh, Miss Judd. Come to discuss additional tutoring hours?"

More time spent listening to him expound on the merit of the sword as the "queen of the weapons"? Heaven spare her. "Actually, a family friend needs your help." She reached behind to grab Gerrett's arm and pull him forward. "He was on the westbound train to Chicago and lost some items in the wreckage."

Gerrett and Professor Goswell shook hands and exchanged names and pleasantries.

"How can I be of assistance?" Professor Goswell asked Gerrett.

"My architectural drawings have gone missing. Since it

looks as if I'll be stranded in Hillsdale for the next week, I'd like to redraw my floor plans."

"President Fairfield," Liberty added, "said you would know where we could find some unused vellum for Mr. Divine to use."

"Unused, no." With a furrowed brow, Professor Goswell closed his journal. "However, I recall Miss Finney mentioning we have leftover printed invitations to the Saint Valentine's Day Social. Could you use them?"

Gerrett nodded. "Merely a matter of wetting the vellum and scraping off the ink."

"Excellent." Professor Goswell then handed Gerrett the antique sword. "Hold this." As he opened the display case, Gerrett twirled the blade and made a thrusting move.

Liberty rolled her eyes. Men and weapons!

"Solid, even weight," Gerrett said. "Ahh, 1300s England?"

"Correct." Professor Goswell took the sword. "Miss Judd, during which phase of the Hundred Years' War did this style of blade emerge as a military weapon?" he asked, replacing the sword in the case.

"The Edwardian Era War, which was followed by the Caroline War nine years later. And the Lancastrian War twenty-six years after it."

"Excellent. Who owned this particular sword?"

"Oliver Ingham, when in support of King Edward, he defended Gascony from French invasion."

All worthless information, really, for her to know, although she did find it fascinating that Oliver Ingham had married a lady who, like him, had been born and raised in the same small English village. She liked to imagine they'd been each other's first and only love. They'd had two girls. The younger married Lord Strange of Knockin. Were he to have been a character in *Macbeth,* Shakespeare would have written: Knock, knock, knock. Who's there, i' the name of Beelzebub? Knockin'. Knockin'? Yes, knockin' is Lord Strange of Knockin.

Who wouldn't enjoy Shakespeare written like that?

Suddenly Gerrett's hand rested on the small of her back. "Edward III."

Liberty blinked, her spine unable to go any straighter. "What?"

Professor Goswell chuckled as he pocketed the key to the display case. "Miss Judd, I asked you which King Edward had Ingham supported, but you were lost in your thoughts again and unable to hear me."

"I was actually pondering *Macbeth*." Which was true. To a degree.

"Lady Principal Whipple will be pleased to know."

Liberty squared her shoulders, despite—certainly not because of—the tingling emanating from the spot where Gerrett's hand still touched her spine. Strange that. "And do be sure to recommend Miss Whipple give me extra credit for pondering Shakespeare outside a class assignment."

Professor Goswell laughed again. What she admired most about him was his good humor and joyfulness, something she rarely saw anymore since he began courting Miss Charmaine Finney. While Miss Finney was a caring and amiable person, she had almost no sense of humor. Professor Goswell ought to have a wife with whom he could jest.

"Of course," she offered, "if *you* wish to give me extra credit, too, for correctly identifying the Edwardian Era, Caroline and Lancastrian Wars, I will not object."

"I take it your grade in literature is near what it is in my class."

Her lips twitched, fighting against a smile. "As long as one considers *near* a matter of perspective."

This time Gerrett joined in with Goswell's laughter.

Liberty gave in to a smug grin. Truly, there was no reason to take offense at their amusement. Her self-value was not in what grade she earned in a class. While she'd come to Hillsdale to escape her parents, the college had become more than a refuge. It was a sanctuary. It was where she fellowshipped with fellow Christians, where she had a chance to learn things she never would on her own with people she would have never met had she stayed in Chicago, in her parents' social class. Mostly, Hillsdale was where she felt free.

"Shall we?" Professor Goswell motioned with his head to the museum door then began walking. "Divine, do you fence?"

As Gerrett answered in the affirmative, Liberty fell into step with him and her professor. The men discussed fencing (their love for it, to be precise), finding the perfect rapier (both insisted owning), and the myriad other swords in the museum, such as the German Kriegsmesser, the Swiss saber, a basket-hilt claymore, scimitars from three different centuries (at this point she began admiring the architecture of the window frames) and the Japanese Wakizashi.

She didn't mind Gerrett finding a friend in Ayden Goswell, but—really, weapons of war? Couldn't they find a more interesting common ground?

Somewhere between extolling the Wakizashi's virtues and finding the vellum invitations in the treasurer's office, Professor Goswell offered Gerrett use of a spare room at his home until the train began running again.

Gerrett hesitated, until Professor Goswell raved over his mother's cooking.

Liberty wanted to remind Gerrett that the Bentzes might have an unoccupied room on the men's floor of the boardinghouse. But then she remembered he had floor plans to draw and a fiancée to propose to. No sense keeping him close to her.

He had a future in Chicago.

And she had a life without him.

Chapter 10

Feeling wearier from Liberty's silence than from the brisk pace she had set upon leaving the campus, Gerrett opened the boardinghouse's front door as a cuckoo clock began chiming the hour. Four o'clock. To think the train wreck had been only sixteen hours ago.

"You should take Goswell up on the extra credit offer." He waited for Liberty to enter before him.

She didn't answer. Neither did she move from her spot next to him on the porch. Her nose was red. Her cheeks, too. The look captivated him. *Liberty* captivated him. If he leaned forward, stretched out his arm, he could pull her into an embrace and kiss her. The urge was overwhelming.

The urge was also untimely and unwise.

Which was why, against his desires, Gerrett propped the door open with his left foot, then nudged Liberty inside and out of the cold. "How taxing would it be?" He closed the door.

"Enough to make me realize how content I am with

my current grade." She swirled around and extended her hand. He placed his gloved hand in hers, and she shook. Vigorously. "It was grand meeting you again, Mr. Divine. I do wish you well on your journey." She released his hand and took a step back as if to say, *Well, go on, leave.*

He should. He had his luggage to collect and transport to the Goswell house. He had vellum in the pocket of his greatcoat that needed to be wet, scraped and dried so he could begin redrawing his house designs in the morning.

Only, he didn't want to go. At least, not yet.

Thus Gerrett looked about the almost empty front room of the boardinghouse to the dining tables, where a young woman with mousy brown hair and tired eyes and wearing a drab woolen dress was sitting, her pencil poised over a journal. Dr. Clark's nurse! The one who had given him tea. She intently watched them, though, instead of writing. A medical bag, a tapestry portmanteau and a charcoal-gray cloak rested on the center of the table.

"My head aches," he muttered, touching his actually still-tender temple.

Liberty gasped. "Oh, I'd forgotten. Let me find—" she spun around "—Katie, you're back. Good!"

Within minutes, Gerrett was sitting at a dining hall table and having his scalp examined by a demure yet competent female *doctor*—Katie Clark. As she and Mrs. Bentz plied him with questions about his day, she (1) cleaned the matted blood from his hair, (2) lectured him on the foolishness of not waiting in the church for a doctor to examine him, (3) asked Mrs. Bentz to make a cold pack, then (4) declared him fortunate that his injury wasn't deep enough to need stitches. The walnut-size knot on his forehead would need to be watched, though.

Sometime during his exam, Liberty found a seat across the table, opposite Gerrett, and began mending the turned-inside-out tweed coat Mr. Emery had dropped off.

Still standing, Dr. Clark put her journal, pencil and medical tools back in her black medical bag while Gerrett held against his temple the bag of packed snow that Mrs. Bentz had given him before returning to the kitchen.

"Who are you sewing for today?" Dr. Clark asked.

"Mr. Emery." Liberty continued to stitch. "We met him this morning on his way to Osseo."

Dr. Clark's brown-eyed gaze shifted from Liberty to Gerrett. "We?"

"Mr. Divine and myself," Liberty answered first. "He's affianced."

"To Miss Uptograss," Gerrett added, albeit more cheerfully than necessary.

Liberty's gaze shifted to the cuckoo clock near the front door. "The Reverend Scott is marrying them today. It's already 4:46 p.m. I'm surprised Mr. Emery isn't back from Osseo."

Gerrett nodded, even though he had no idea how long Emery would need to bring his fiancée to Hillsdale. Or why the man hadn't thought to find a preacher in Osseo to perform the vows. His forehead cold, he lowered the bag of packed snow, only for Dr. Clark to immediately raise his hand and the bag back to his forehead.

Dr. Clark then slid sideways onto the table's bench, half facing Liberty, half facing Gerrett. "Correct me if I'm wrong. Mr. Divine here is not the one engaged to Miss Uptograss?"

Liberty laughed and spoke before Gerrett could. "No, Gerrett is soon to be engaged to Mrs. Ann Bartlett of Chicago." She moistened the end of the thread between her lips and rethreaded her needle. "Mr. Emery received a telegram this morning from Miss Uptograss, accepting his proposal."

"Now that makes sense," Dr. Clark answered.

Liberty looked to Gerrett, her light blue-gray eyes

twinkling. She looked radiant. The urge to kiss her returned.

As she leaned forward, her voice softened as if she were sharing a secret. "He proposed to her before I moved to Hillsdale, and she said she needed time to answer. It's been over two years."

Although there were only three of them in the dining hall, Gerrett couldn't help leaning forward, too, and whispering, "Why?"

"She has three cats," came Liberty's sober reply. She turned Emery's coat outside out and began stitching the inside seam she'd loosened.

Assured she was jesting him, he looked to Dr. Clark, who more soberly shared, "He has five cats of his own."

Looking back and forth between them, Gerrett waited for a telltale lift to the corners of their mouths, or a glint of amusement in their eyes, or even a betraying giggle. Nothing. They were completely serious. Or skilled actresses. Still, he had no response.

The thought of being the immediate mother of *eight* cats, he concluded, would be more than enough of a reason for any woman to take over two years to accept a marriage proposal. At least Miss Uptograss liked cats. She apparently decided she liked eight of them. What never ceased to amaze him were the number of people who adored felines yet couldn't conceive how everyone else didn't share their adoration.

"Suum cuique," he muttered.

Dr. Clark laughed. "My sentiments exactly."

Liberty groaned. "Ugh, Latin. Translate, please."

"Do you not study at all?" Dr. Clark asked. After Liberty shrugged noncommittally, she explained, "It is the short form of *suum cuique pulchrum est.*"

"To each his own is beautiful," Gerrett translated.

While Liberty was distractingly beautiful to him,

after walking around with her today, he suspected several male Hillsdale students and villagers felt the same, beyond George Quackenbush, Mr. Emery and the Reverend Scott. He also suspected Liberty enjoyed being admired as much as she disliked the attention being admired brought her.

"Suum cuique." The words rolled off Liberty's tongue with the perfect Latin inflection. "Hmm. I may be able to earn some extra credit points in Latin using that in every day tête-à-tête."

"Or you could study," Dr. Clark interjected, "and thereby not need to rely on extra credit to pass the class."

"It's Latin, Katie. Let the dead stay dead."

"Why did you take French *and* Latin in the same semester?" Gerrett asked.

"I told her not to. Lady Principal Whipple told her not to."

Liberty resumed sewing. "Two birds, one stone."

"That's not—" Gerrett looked to Dr. Clark, who shook her head in warning. Since his forehead was numb, he removed the snow pack and rested it on the table. This time Dr. Clark didn't direct him otherwise. "I like dogs," he said for no clear reason.

"Ann Bartlett has a Sleeve Pekingese." Liberty stopped sewing. Her grin turned mischievous, which only flared his yearning to kiss her again. "Perhaps you should propose by way of telegram."

"Oh!" Dr. Clark shuffled the fabric of her blue skirt until she found a pocket. She withdrew a handful of yellow papers. "That new gentleman who assists Charlie in the telegraph—"

"Homer Smith?" Liberty supplied.

"Yes. Why can't I ever remember his name? I never have a problem remembering anyone else's."

"Because you memorize what you first see and don't

adjust for variables. Mr. Smith is a living variable—" Liberty grimaced "—an algebraic problem you can't solve. Sometimes he wears spectacles, sometimes doesn't. When his hair is oiled, it looks brown. When it's not, it's blond. His voice occasionally has an accent."

"Quite perceptive of you to notice," Gerrett mused, instantly disliking Homer Smith.

Liberty grinned. "Thank you."

For someone who disliked learning, she was quite astute. He'd wager that she merely believed she wasn't smart enough to learn, or had been told she wasn't.

Gerrett turned to Dr. Clark. "Doesn't it make you wonder how she deduced that about Mr. Smith, yet never noticed Mr. Emery's *tendre?*"

Dr. Clark nodded. "I told her—"

"Mr. Emery is affianced," Liberty said in exasperation.

Gerrett was about to respond—after all, Liberty couldn't be allowed to get away with such a weasely answer—but then she glared at him.

"Homer Smith is no conquest, either."

Dr. Clark regarded them suspiciously. "Liberty, is there something I should know?" Gerrett caught the implied *about you two?*

"Mr. Divine is jealous."

Gerrett let out a short laugh to cover how right Liberty was. "Apparently, a good number of bachelors in this town are enamored with Miss Judd."

"I've mentioned this to her before," Dr. Clark replied. "Seems she needs to listen more to her friends."

Liberty ignored him and instead looked warmly at her roommate. "Katie, if you stop trying to solve what puzzles you about Mr. Smith, the truth is obvious. He's hiding his real identity."

"How did you reach that conclusion?"

"I despise math," she said, obviously proud of her disdain, "thus I take him for what he appears to be."

Dr. Clark frowned as if she wasn't quite sure what to make of that comment. She then tossed the folded papers in front of Liberty. "Mr. Smith saw me at the hospital and asked me to let you know several telegrams had arrived. Since I was headed here, I thought I'd spare you a trip."

To Gerrett's surprise, Liberty resumed stitching and didn't look at any of the telegrams.

Her actions surprised her friend, too. "Aren't you going to read them?"

"You can."

"I already did." With a weary breath, Dr. Clark shifted on the bench to directly face Liberty. "The telegrams are all from your father. Why does he want you to return to Chicago by Monday?" Her eyes were as filled with concern as her tone. "More important, why is he threatening to come here to get you if you don't?"

Liberty's gaze stayed on her stitching. "My parents have chosen a man for me to marry. I won't do it, and now Father thinks he can march over to Hillsdale and pick up Doormat Liberty, and I'll quietly go along."

"Will you?"

Her stitching stopped. She suddenly looked fragile. Scared. Alone. Only she wasn't. He was here. He would help her. He would rescue her and be her shield. That's what friends did for one another. And if she would look up at him, he'd convey that in a glance. No, he'd speak it.

And Gerrett knew, if he did, she would graciously not accept.

"Oh, Katie, I don't know," she said weakly. "I've never stood up to my father. No one *ever* stands up to him."

She held the coat to the side and gave it a flick, causing two loose threads to flutter to the table. She folded the coat and laid it to the side.

"I have enough money saved to last the semester." She looked at Dr. Clark. "All the assistance jobs at local businesses are filled by other college students. I doubt Sheriff Dawes would hire me to be a deputy due to the encumbrance of my gender, not to mention my inability to ride a horse or shoot a gun, although I would not mind learning both. Do you really think I could make a go of a sewing business?"

Yes! Gerrett would have yelled if she had asked him. She could do anything if she put her mind to it. He had to convince her of that. He had to prove to her she was more than she thought she was. Gerrett opened his mouth, but before he could speak, Dr. Clark placed her palm against the back of his hand, silencing him. She drew back.

"Yes, Lib," she answered in a tender voice. "I know you can. Everyone you help free of charge always offers to pay you, anyway. The real question is, why are *you* hesitant to do it?"

Liberty replaced her scissors, needle and thread in her sewing basket. The desperate, practical side of her that didn't want to return to Chicago and live under her father's heel anymore screamed at her to agree with Katie.

"I don't want to be paid for doing good deeds," she answered.

"I get paid to do good deeds."

"You're a doctor."

"I'll be your first customer," Katie offered. "Let me pay you for the gown you're making me for the Saint Valentine's Day Social."

"But you bought the fabric and supplies."

"Yes, and I should pay for the sewing, too. I want to."

Liberty looked from Katie to Gerrett. His slight smile made something in her chest tighten. He'd help her if she asked—she knew that with confidence. But she couldn't accept his help. And she knew he knew it.

"All right. In the morning I'll go to the mercantile and post an advertisement."

"An advertisement?" Ursula said, entering the dining hall with a plate of sliced rye bread and a steaming bowl of vegetable soup. Her skirt bustled as she crossed the floor. "For what?"

"Miss Judd is starting a sewing business," Gerrett answered matter-of-factly.

Ursula set the bowl and plate in front of Gerrett, then withdrew a spoon and knife from her apron pocket and handed them to him. "Eat. Josef is ready to take you to the Goswells' house, but you are welcome here anytime. I will feed you, *ja?*"

Gerrett ate a spoonful of soup. *"Ja,"* he repeated. "Thank you."

Ursula cast her slant-eyed gaze upon Liberty. Of what she was trying to convey this time, Liberty had no idea. She gave Ursula a *what?* look back. Only Ursula shook her head and continued on to the kitchen.

"I need to go, too." Katie stood and pulled on her woolen capelike coat, buttoning it closed. "Joshua and Father are waiting for me."

Joshua? Liberty didn't know anyone in Hillsdale by that name. "Who's Joshua?"

A blush stole across Katie's cheeks. "You mean you haven't heard the gossip?"

"No." She inclined her head toward Gerrett. "I've been helping him."

"Liberty, I have so much I need to tell you, but tending to the wounded has taken all my time of late. Joshua is claiming he's my fiancé."

"Oh. Is he?"

"It's…complicated." Katie grabbed her portmanteau

and medical bag, one in each hand. She stepped around the table.

"Where are you going?" Liberty asked.

"I need to stay at Father's house until he recovers. I'll come over tomorrow after I do my morning rounds at the hospital." She strolled to the front door, calling over her shoulder, "Be sure and buy an ad in the newspaper, too, and don't forget to study for your theology and French tests on Monday. I expect at least Cs on both this time."

As Katie left, several college students, including the Quackenbush twins, arrived for the evening meal. Fred glared at Gerrett, yet said nothing. Everyone else acknowledged Liberty and Gerrett with a cordial greeting.

After cleaning up her sewing supplies, Liberty left Gerrett to finish his soup and went upstairs to return her sewing basket to the suite she shared with Katie. Next to her old sewing machine was the new Singer she'd ordered to replace the old one that Katie continually insisted she sell. She'd intended to, but now that she was opening a business, owning two machines was practical.

On the floor between the two machines was a stack of clothes to alter for the Miller family. The periwinkle gown she had sewn for Olive Wittingham lay across her bed. The mint-green silk brocade gown she was sewing for Katie hung on the mannequin near the window.

As if the "dressed" mannequin beckoned her, she walked to it. She ran her fingers along the woven rose pattern in the fabric. Katie needed another fitting, in a crinoline and with shoes this time.

"I can't take money from my friends," she muttered. But she had to. Her choice was to sew for a living or return to Chicago and agree to Father's demands. Or she could marry someone in Hillsdale. No, that wasn't an option.

Next to her bed were her textbooks and class notes. If she didn't improve her grades in French and natural theology, she wouldn't be allowed to attend the spring quarter. Lady Principal Whipple's warning had been clear enough. There wasn't enough extra credit for her to earn to compensate for the French tests she continued to fail. She needed help. What if she asked Gerrett? He was fluent in the language. Clearly they had come to a place where they were like minds in regards to their relationship—or agreed-upon lack thereof.

Friends helped one another.

Her heart flipped in her chest. Not with desire like it had since she spotted him at the train wreckage, but with joy and with hope. He would help her...and expect nothing in return.

Liberty grabbed her French book and study notes and hurried back downstairs. The dining hall was full and noisy, everyone eating, and the sole person she wanted to see was nowhere to be seen.

She opened her study notes. The foreign words made no more sense to her than algebra. She needed help. Desperately.

Going to the Goswells' home was out of the question because her history professor would interpret her appearance as agreement to his extra credit option. As much as she appreciated the offer, she was *not* going to spend two hours watching Ayden Goswell and Gerrett fence while they explained the importance of sword fighting in warfare and its evolution into the sport of modern fencing. Besides, Gerrett had his architectural drawings to recreate. However, if she just so happened to see him about town tomorrow—not that she would be looking—she'd ask for his tutoring assistance.

In the meantime, she'd study. On her own. By choice.

Liberty refocused on the study questions. Her mouth

suddenly held a sour taste, so she closed her journal. Tomorrow she'd study.

Tonight she had an advertisement for her new business to create.

Chapter 11

Saturday arrived with cloudy skies and promises of more snow. Yet none came.

After a restless night's sleep, Liberty assisted Ursula with breakfast, then went to the mercantile to post her sewing advertisement.

On her walk to the hospital to deliver fresh-baked pumpkin muffins to the train-wreck victims, she stopped at the depot and picked up another telegram from her father. Homer Smith was arriving for his shift and Charlie was leaving, so she gave a muffin to both men while sharing that she would no longer be doing alterations for them—or anyone for that matter—free of charge. The time had come for her to open a sewing business.

Mr. Smith said it was about time. Charlie insisted on paying her a dollar for her last set of alterations. And *I'm sorry* was uttered six times during the conversation—five by Liberty and the last by Charlie, who hadn't understood something Homer Smith had said and needed it repeated.

Liberty considered asking Mr. Smith how it was he sometimes had a Scottish—Irish?—accent, but she chose not to expose his secret. Not that she knew what his secret exactly was; nonetheless, she was respecting his privacy.

Leaving Mr. Smith to attend to the telegraph, Liberty visited the hospital. Between handing out the muffins and giving the dollar from Charlie to the hospital to cover the expenses of an indigent father, Mr. Knapp, she spoke and prayed with each victim.

Two hours later, she returned to the unusually quiet boardinghouse. A note left by Ursula said she and Josef would be out delivering food to train-wreck victims. Olive arrived to pick up her repaired dress. Tears of joy broke Olive's composure. She immediately began digging through her well-worn handbag for coins to pay, even though Liberty knew Olive earned very little doing laundry at the hotel.

To distract her friend, Liberty immediately brought up the Reverend Burton Scott, which made Olive stop digging for money and complain about unrequited love, which led to Liberty's confession about Gerrett Divine, which switched into a discussion on how both their lives would be easier without men in them, which resulted in their vowing to a life of spinsterhood.

The last part may have been more for dramatic purposes than any truthful avowal.

Liberty eventually managed to usher Olive and Samuel out the boardinghouse front door without Olive realizing she'd failed to pay. Sometimes a girl had to choose to do good for others even if it cost her financially. Especially for people in need.

Especially for people God tells a girl to bless.

At approximately 11:23 a.m., Liberty attended Mr. Emery's wedding to Miss Uptograss at First Church. Following a hearty toast and a slice of wedding cake, Liberty searched for Katie to ask her about the mysterious Joshua. She wasn't at the hospital or the Clark residence. And her father, Dr. Ethan Clark, was sleeping and unable to answer questions. Last his housekeeper, Mrs. Holden, knew was Katie and her fiancé were heading over to the boardinghouse.

Liberty returned to where she'd begun her day and encountered the aftermath caused by a simple kiss between her roommate and the mysterious Joshua. Katie could no longer live in the boardinghouse. If Lady Principal Whipple was willing to forbid college students to board with the Bentzes until Katie married Joshua McCain, then what would she do if she found out Gerrett had kissed *her* and they weren't even supposedly engaged?

Liberty climbed the stairs to her lonely, empty room. Katie had been her roommate from the first day Liberty had moved to Hillsdale four months ago. Who was she to have her usual evening heart-to-heart chat with?

First, she read her Bible.

Then she prayed through everything on her prayer list.

Finally, she opened her copy of William Paley's *Natural Theology: or, Evidences of the Existence and Attributes of the Deity collected from the Appearances of Nature.* She read several pages before realizing she was staring absently at the top paragraph on page twenty-three and not comprehending anything. Despite her ardent faith, theology was as dead a subject to her as Latin. At this point she was going to have to rely on knowing short answers because her expository essays would be… Well, at least she'd earn points for penmanship and grammar.

She put her book aside. "God, the more I study about how the different theologians try to explain You, the more I realize how much of a mystery You are." She leaned against the bed's headboard. "You are in reach of my heart, but not of my mind. You are a paradox. And I am all right with that."

Rested in her spirit, she climbed off the bed.

After digging through her cedar chest to find a length of flannel, she laid a pattern she'd made for her oldest nephew on the floor atop the plaid and cut out a shirt for Samuel Knapp. She replaced the firewood in her warming stove twice during the hours she sewed and stitched the garment. As her eyes began to droop, she finished sewing on the last button.

Liberty doused her lamps and, content with her evening's work, climbed into bed for the night. For the first time in the past seven years, she had spent a day not obsessing over Gerrett Henry Divine IV.

She smiled.

Then her gaze fell upon the stack of telegrams from her father. For now, she'd let tomorrow worry itself.

Sunday arrived with cloudy skies and more promises of snow. Yet none came. Thankfully. But what snow had arrived the night of the train wreck still remained, although the rooftops and sidewalks had been swept clear.

Liberty sat in the middle of the campus chapel, wishing she were attending worship with the Bentzes and Katie. The Reverends Scott and Quinn always delivered exceptional sermons when she worshipped at First Church. But after running into the Reverend Scott twice yesterday, and seeing the hurt in his eyes, she felt the kindest thing she could do was not attend his service and risk being a distraction to him.

While her fellow Hillsdale students filled the chapel, she dutifully rested a hymnal in the lap of her amethyst silk gown and flipped through it, looking for the song Lady Principal Whipple was playing not too perfectly on the organ. The Reverend Dunn and President Fairfield took their seats on the stage.

President Fairfield caught her eye and nodded.

She dipped her chin in acknowledgment of his approval. After receiving his warning, she knew she ought to follow with diligence the deportment regulations, especially the one on church and chapel attendance. If she was going to be expelled from Hillsdale, it'd be for her failure to comprehend French and not because of any failure adhering to rules of conduct. Nor would she do anything to cause anyone to look disfavorably on the Bentzes.

"Who's that couple with Professor Goswell and Miss Finney?" a female in the pew behind her whispered rather loudly.

"I hope they're brother and sister," came another voice, also not loud enough for Liberty to recognize who was speaking. "He's a regular Prince Charming. Scoot over and let me sit with you."

"Hey," a third girl piped in, "that's the guy I saw in the sleigh with Liberty. Let me in, too."

"Can't be. I heard the guy with Liberty was quite taken with her." The first girl groaned. "That's my foot you stepped on."

"Sorry. She deserves someone better than George Quackenbush, that's for sure."

A gasp, then, "Is that Liberty two rows in front of us?"

"Can't be. She has permission to attend First Church with—"

"Shh, service is starting."

"Quick, give me a hymnal. Whipple is staring at us."

Her heartbeat increasing its pace, Liberty took her time to look up from the hymnal in her lap to the organ, where Lady Principal Whipple was *indeed* staring in their direction. She turned from Miss Whipple to spy a well-dressed couple sitting next to Professor Goswell and Charmaine Finney in the second row of the chapel, organ side.

The chestnut-haired woman in an exquisite blue floral gown said something to Professor Goswell. He then spoke to Miss Finney, who was wearing the triple-tier-skirted, silk-and-wool dress Liberty had altered for her last month. The man with them looked over his shoulder.

Liberty's breath caught. Gerrett?

His gaze searched the chapel looking for—

His eyes caught hers, and he smiled. She smiled, too. Her insides also flipped and fluttered and felt all warm and tingly like when he'd kissed her. She didn't touch her lips even though *they* now felt all warm and tingly. Was she blushing? She had to be blushing. Besides Lady Principal Whipple, who knew who else was watching her and wondering what had caused her to blush.

Liberty bowed her head.

Her pulse continued to race. How did Gerrett know she was here? He couldn't have. Even if he'd asked Goswell, he wouldn't have known to look for her. Everyone in Hillsdale knew the second Sunday of the month was the day she had permission from President Fairfield and Lady Principal Whipple to attend worship at First Church with Katie and the Bentzes instead of attending the mandatory Hillsdale church service.

Yet he *had* looked for her.

As if he knew she was here.

As if he could *feel* she was in the same room with him.

Unsettled by the thought, she pinched her eyes and focused her attention on the words her theology professor was praying. She needed to focus on Jesus.

Gerrett sat patiently through the service, first sharing a hymnal then a Bible with Miss Euphemia Roper while she cradled in her lap the bandaged wrist she had wounded in the train wreck. When she'd asked him to allow her to sit on the end of the pew, he'd intentionally pretended not to hear her request so she would have to sit next to Goswell. Not that Gerrett had a problem sitting next to another man. It was merely a matter of compassion.

The tension between Miss Roper and Goswell yesterday had been sharper than the wrong key the organist hit during the opening hymn this morning. That—the tension, not the discordant music—rather annoyed Gerrett, who'd been trying to concentrate on his drawings but ended up watching the pair bicker.

He'd spoken with Goswell's mother and discovered the truth. Her son had fallen in love with Miss Roper a year and a half ago when they both were attending Michigan Central College, the forerunner to Hillsdale. Goswell had even proposed. Yet Miss Roper had chosen to follow her journalistic career over love. Over Goswell.

Being second priority in the life of the woman one loved was enough to make any man on edge when in her presence. Not to mention angry, hurt and resentful.

No matter how devoted Goswell was to Miss Charmaine Finney, Gerrett suspected what the professor felt for the department chairman's daughter couldn't be more than kindly affection. Yet with Miss Roper—the sparks were so sharp Gerrett could feel them.

As far as he was concerned, making the pair sit next to each other in church was an act of compassion on his part. Mostly for Miss Finney. She would make any man a splendid wife. According to Mrs. Goswell, her son was planning on proposing soon to Miss Finney. Being someone himself who was drawn to one woman yet about to be engaged to another, he knew Ayden Goswell and Euphemia Roper needed to confront their feelings before Goswell pledged his life to Miss Finney.

As I should face with mine for Liberty.

The past two days apart from her had only increased the connection with her that he felt. From the moment he woke, she'd been a constant in his mind. He could feel her presence even at this moment. He had since he'd stepped inside the chapel.

Gerrett uttered an unmanly sigh.

Miss Roper looked at him questioningly.

He needed to say something to Liberty. No, he needed to avoid her. But she would want to know how his drawings were coming along. That spark between them needed to be avoided. No, a connection wasn't a spark. What he felt was friendship. Pure and simple. And as a friend he would say something to her and then return to the Goswell house to resume his designs, but not kiss her.

Never again.

Gerrett uttered another unmanly sigh.

Miss Roper patted his knee with a silent *there, there, it'll be all right.*

As soon as the benediction came to an end, Gerrett jumped to his feet. "If you will pardon me, Miss Roper, I see a friend I need to speak to."

Her green eyes widened, face paled a fraction. She cast a nervous glance at Goswell and the golden beauty named Charmaine Finney, who, like Goswell, was still sitting. Miss Roper looked back at Gerrett, her features all composed.

"Take as long as you need, Mr. Divine. I can see myself back to the house.

"Pish posh, Miss Roper," Miss Finney said, now standing and smiling. "You must join us for Sunday dinner. Cloretta is making her prized dumpling stew."

"Thank you, but Mrs. Goswell is expecting my assistance with dinner."

Miss Finney rested a hand on her bodice, right above

her heart. "Here is where I must seek your forgiveness. Yesterday I asked Mrs. Goswell if I could steal you and Ayden away this afternoon. She agreed. The selfish side of me is dying to hear anything you can tell me about Boston. Please say yes."

There was a pause.

Then Miss Roper nodded.

Not the kind of nod that says *I am happy to oblige*. Instead, the kind that says *Oh fine, I'll do it because you are such a sweet person and I like you, despite the fact you are courting the man I once loved.*

Gerrett would pity Goswell, but why? The man was caught between two beautiful and kindhearted women. He needed to make a choice.

Miss Finney turned her heavily lashed blue eyes upon Gerrett. "Give my regards to Miss Judd."

How did she know who he intended to speak to?

Before he could question her, she said, "I generally don't heed gossip. However, if any woman deserves a man to shower her with devotion, that woman is Liberty Judd. Her willingness to help those in need inspires me to be more selfless in my giving." She waved him away. "Go on, Mr. Divine. Your lady is waiting."

Liberty wasn't his lady. She couldn't be. He was marrying someone else, and even if he weren't, Liberty wouldn't have him even if he asked. Their paths faced different directions.

Gerrett nodded to acknowledge Miss Finney's words. He then casually worked his way through the throng of students.

He met Liberty at the coatroom's entrance. "Here, let me." He took her cloak—the same green velvet one with the fur-lined hood he'd seen her in on the night of the train wreck—from her and draped it over her shoulders.

"You look like a canary-filled cat," she remarked, buttoning her cloak.

"I like mornings," Gerrett said—because he actually did like them—then went to claim his greatcoat. His gaze searched the filled racks.

"I've heard one county in Michigan considers that a virtue," came from outside the coatroom.

"What's a virtue?"

"Liking mornings."

Gerrett grabbed his coat and hat then tossed them on. He exited the coatroom. "Which county?"

"Does it matter? I will never be invited." She was watching him with a tilt to her head. "I take it you are escorting me back to the boardinghouse."

"I'm dutiful like that."

"That's all I am to you—a duty?"

Her directness unhinged him, killing his amusement. She wasn't a duty to him. She was… She had to be…

"A friend."

She nodded—just a little, just enough for him to realize she was accepting of his answer. She drew her hood over her head. "I need to help Ursula with the noon meal."

He pulled on his gloves and made sure Liberty had on her calfskin ones before they stepped outside. Since she didn't seem bothered by the silence as they strolled down the snow-packed street, he elected to not be, either.

But he was bothered. More by the chill between them than the chill in the air.

How could he say he wanted her to be a friend to him when he didn't know himself what he wanted? Or what he felt. The day he stepped on the ship in the Le Havre seaport, he knew he (1) loved God, his family, dogs, architecture, fencing and crisp butter cookies, (2) wanted to leave a legacy, (3) was willing to marry Ann because his parents had asked him to, (4) yearned to open a design firm and (5)—

"Gerrett, why are you muttering numbers?"

—he wasn't a person who trusted in feelings. He wasn't a romantic. Nor had he ever been a love-struck, poetry-writing, cupid-believing fool. He expected he would make a practical marriage, and then, as his parents and grandparents had done, he would fall in love with his wife. They would have children, and everything would be good and right and well in his world.

"Gerrett?" Liberty pressed.

He turned his head just enough to regard her as they walked. Her lips curved in what he knew she meant to be a smile, but it wasn't. Not quite.

"Numbers?" he asked.

"Yes, you counted to five."

"I make lists when I'm frustrated."

She thought about that for a moment. "That is... strange."

"Counting? Or my being frustrated?"

She just smiled. A real smile.

He took her hand and placed it around the crook of his arm. "Worship was enjoyable."

Liberty nodded. "Miss Finney looked ravishing."

"She's a gracious lady."

"Who was the woman sitting between you and Professor Goswell?"

Gerrett quickly explained who Miss Roper was and how she came to be staying along with other train-wreck passengers at the Goswells' home. Then, as they were within sight of the boardinghouse, he shared about the tension he'd felt yesterday between Euphemia Roper and Ayden Goswell and what Mrs. Goswell had confessed.

"What?" Liberty stopped him from walking, and her hand fell from his arm. Her eyes were wide, whether with dread or surprise he wasn't sure. "He once proposed to Miss Roper? Are you truthful? Oh, of course you would be truthful," she muttered. "You would never lie to me."

"Unless I had good cause," he said without expression.

She gave him a peeved look. "Such as?"

Gerrett chuckled. He couldn't help himself. "If we were on a boat that was sinking in the middle of the Mississippi, with sharks circling us, and there was no way we were going to survive, I would still tell you that we would be all right."

One of her brows lifted. "Sharks do not live in rivers, although there are a few known exceptions, such as the bull shark and the river shark, which can survive in both seawater and freshwater."

"I thought you didn't like biology."

"I don't. Occasionally, pointless information finds a home in my brainbox. It's rather annoying at times."

The tip of her nose had reddened from the cold. Lovely, charming and forthright to her core—this was the Liberty Adele Judd that had found a home in his brainbox. And she was focused on him, as if they were the only people on the sidewalk...and they weren't. *But* if they were, he knew with certainty he would (1) kiss her and (2) break her heart again.

"One...two," Liberty said. "Will there be a three to this list? Or are you finished?"

With the connection he felt to her? He had to be.

Friends, that's all they were.

"I've been thinking..." Gerrett wrapped Liberty's arm around his. "I want you to take Goswell up on his extra credit offer."

"Wanting that is most gallant of you."

"Is that a bit of sarcasm I hear?"

"No. More like a lump."

Gerrett wasn't dismayed by her lack of enthusiasm.

"It's three easy steps to boost a letter grade. (1) Watch us fence, (2) listen to his lecture, then (3) write an essay on what you learned."

He doubted she tried at all to hide that unladylike growl under her breath.

"I'll think about it," she conceded.

Chapter 12

By the time they stepped inside the boardinghouse, Liberty knew exactly what to do about the extra credit offer: nothing.

With smells of turkey roasting and bread baking filling the dining hall, Ursula set a bowl of rolls on the last table. She waved at them then hurried back into the kitchen.

Liberty took Gerrett's outer garments and laid them along with her cloak on a parlor chair. Troubled, she closed her eyes. *Help me, Lord. With Gerrett and studying and my parents and...*

She continued praying until her tension left.

When she exited the parlor, Gerrett was in the center of the room, taking a tray of salt and pepper shakers from Ursula and nodding at her.

Once the train was running again, he would leave. That, Liberty knew for certain. How could he so easily sacrifice self for his family's greater good? Because he was a Divine. Duty, honor, chivalry ruled—no, guided his life. No wonder his parents were proud of him. Not only that, but the man was fluent in French, and she couldn't properly conjugate the four simple tenses, four moods and six persons of the verb *pouvoir*.

There wasn't a better husband for Ann. But Liberty couldn't deny that the thought of Ann and Gerrett happy together disturbed her. Surely he didn't need to marry Ann to learn the family business. Surely he hadn't kissed Liberty for no other reason than a momentary lapse of judgment. Surely he had some attraction to her. Fondness, even. Perhaps a bit of desire.

Maybe what rankled wasn't that she was jealous of Ann—or that she still loved Gerrett—but that *if* she gave Gerrett any indication that she was interested in courtship, then he could actually pursue her, instead of Ann.

Liberty shook her head.

Even if he loved her and wanted to marry, she wouldn't go back into Chicago society. Puppet, mannequin—either way, her parents wanted her under their influence. Never asking what *she* wanted. Always demanding she submit. Or manipulating her with shame or obligation to sway her to do what they wanted. Once she'd found new life in Christ, her parents—whose faith consisted of nothing more than being able to recite the Ten Commandments, despite how many they broke—had latched on to "children, obey your parents" as a means to extort the behavior they wanted.

Unlike Gerrett, she couldn't so easily sacrifice self for her family's greater good. Not that she could see any greater good in giving control of her future over to her parents.

They'd take advantage of her.

Come tomorrow when her father arrived— Well, he likely wouldn't because of the train not running, so she had a few days' reprieve from having to face the paternal music. That he would arrive was certain. That she would cower to his demands was certain, too.

Of course, she could always flee Hillsdale like she had fled Chicago. No, that was a childish response. Somehow between now and when her father arrived, she had to grow a steel backbone. If she wanted to stay in college, she had to figure out how to improve her grades in French, theology, history and Latin. Truth be admitted, her grade wasn't impressive in literature, either.

"Gerrett," she said.

Ursula stopped speaking to him and returned to the kitchen.

He turned, met her gaze and didn't move. She couldn't stop staring. They were two table-lengths apart, and yet she felt as if she could touch him. The intensity in his blue eyes stole her breath away.

I love you. She yearned to speak it, except the mere thinking of it made her dizzy. Or…maybe what shifted her equilibrium was the knowledge that giving her all to love *wasn't* who she wanted to be anymore. She couldn't survive on loving a man as being what defined her.

She wanted to be defined by duty and honor and chivalry. She wanted to be gracious and strong. She wanted to be more than what she was…. Beginning with not failing college.

"If I don't pass French," she blurted, "I will be expelled. The action would be only fair considering my other grades are less than stellar."

"I'll tutor you."

"You need to redraw your designs."

"It's nothing but a house. This is your future."

"I'm not the best student."

"You are smarter than you give yourself credit for."

The way he looked at her, she knew he cared more about helping her than with recreating the perfect engagement gift. Why did it hurt to accept his help? Because she had never accepted anyone's generosity. She always insisted on paying. Always demanded to have her own way. Always ordering people about.

I am like my father.

The realization was nauseating.

People could change. *She* could change.

Her throat tightened. "I love helping others, but I feel awkward when someone does something for me."

Gerrett slowly nodded, his expression nonjudgmental. "Why do you feel awkward?"

"I don't know."

"For someone who is as candid as you, that's a cowardly answer.

Liberty gritted her teeth. Yes, it was a cowardly answer, because the truth was— She blinked at the warm tears in her eyes. The truth was doing for others made her feel valued, needed. Important. Things she hadn't received from her father in years.

"I feel unworthy of being served." She felt like he could see through to the real Liberty, the part that wasn't nice or likable. Certainly not lovable.

He shifted the platter of salt and pepper shakers to his left hand. "Liberty, to be someone who truly gives selflessly, you have to learn to accept another's offer of help."

"I don't know how to do that."

"Begin with not being selfish. Don't rob me of the joy of serving you."

Was she being selfish?

She felt a nudge from God. She was being selfish.

Liberty winced. Having Gerrett confront her was one thing. Having God confirm Gerrett's confrontation cut deep. She took a breath and released it slowly. She could change. She would.

"I accept your help."

He motioned with his head for her to walk over to him, and she did.

"First, let's assist Mrs. Bentz." Gerrett offered her a pewter salt and pepper set. *"Pour toi, mademoiselle."*

"Oui, s'il vous plait."

As they worked, Liberty listened to Gerrett name the various items in the dining hall, quiz her on the previous items each time after he added a new one and correct her pronunciation. For the first time in four months, she enjoyed speaking French.

Two hours later they collected all the shakers then cleaned the dinner remains from the tables and assisted Ursula with cleaning the kitchen. When finished, they sat at a dining hall table while numerous boardinghouse residents milled about the room. The next lesson was on note-taking tips to help her study better. While enjoying spiced cider, Liberty listened to him explain the basics of the language. She even took notes as he showed her tricks to conjugating the regular and irregular verbs.

She thought about mentioning deportment rule #3: *Ladies may receive gentlemen callers in the general parlor of the house they are residing, and such calls may be made only during recreation hours on weekdays between 3:00 and 7:00 p.m.* However, since Gerrett was only tutoring her, no one would define him as a gentleman caller.

"Next on your list is *cacher,*" Gerrett said, "which means…?"

She propped her elbow on the table, rested her chin in her hand and studied him. His left eyebrow had a scar through it, like someone had—

"Liberty?" He waved his hand in front of her face. "You've stopped listening to me, haven't you?"

She felt her cheeks warm. "I'm sorry."

She looked to her study notes to see which verb they were on next. *Cacher.* Fitting because that's why she was at Hillsdale—hiding from her parents. Even when she was a child she used to hide in the—

"House," she said with a gasp.

His gaze fell from her eyes to her lips. Then he abruptly looked away, clearing his throat. "Ahh, house is not a verb. *Cacher* means to hide. The tenses are…?"

As excitement increased her pulse, she covered her study notes with both hands. "When I was a child, I used to sit in the window seat and draw the curtains over it so I could hide from my family. All children should have places to hide. Nooks and crannies. Secret doors under the stairs."

A crease deepened between his brows. "And that relates to verb conjugation how?"

"Oh, not at all," she said happily. "I think you should add hiding places to your house design. Your duty is to have children, *n'est-ce pas?*"

Technically, his wife would be doing the child-having.

Gerrett nodded. He wanted children. A dozen. Maybe not a dozen. Six would be fine. Or even three. All boys. All girls. Half and half. Forty-sixty. Ninety-ten.

And they could learn French or not learn French. He'd love them and he'd love their mother and he'd teach his children to love God, and someday he'd tell them how he fell in love with their mother by way of a train wreck. Liberty, of course, would respond with sharing how he'd injured his head and had spoken like a madman all priggish and snow-covered, which would make their children laugh. Then he'd laugh, and she'd laugh, and he'd think how complete his life was. Someday. After she married him.

Because they were together.

Because he married her instead of Ann.

"No—yes—no," he muttered.

Liberty looked at him oddly. "Which is it?"

He looked down at the study notes, the words blurring together, his head aching with confusion. He didn't want to marry Liberty. That he was drawn to her was undeniable. They had a connection. But marriage? She wouldn't agree even if he proposed, and he had no intention of doing so.

He had a life in Chicago. She…didn't.

Different paths, he reminded himself.

Pained in his chest, Gerrett grabbed his mug and finished the chilled and now-unappealing remains of his spiced cider. He put his empty mug down. "Children are in my future."

Liberty turned her head toward the cuckoo clock then gasped. "I forgot all about Samuel." She closed her books and stacked them together then stood. "I need to deliver a package before it gets dark."

He stood. "I'll escort you."

"It's to the hospital."

"The Goswells live two blocks from there."

Liberty reached for his hand and gave it a little squeeze. "Thank you for the tutoring. And for being a friend."

She ran upstairs, leaving his hand empty and the room listless and dull.

Gerrett stared aimlessly at the table, for how long he didn't know, until he could calm his racing thoughts.

The intensity of what he felt for Liberty couldn't be love. Love didn't grow in three days. Love took months, years even. Love was more than the desire he had for her. It was— It had to be— A maelstrom of emotions. How had Leonidas described it two months ago? The realization that as long as you live, your life will never be your own again. He exhaled in exasperation.

If that were love, he couldn't fathom it being enjoyable.

By the time he had collected their coats, Liberty returned with a package. Properly bundled, they walked to the hospital, her arm wrapped around his…by *her* choosing, not his. Last thing he wanted at this moment was any physical connection with her.

Liberty quizzed him about his designs, complimented his arrangement of rooms and then reminded him of Ann Bartlett's favorite colors. The thought of what was expected of him weighed on Gerrett's soul.

He maintained a cheerful disposition with her and with those in the hospital, yet the reality of his future seemed to tighten its grip on the joy he'd felt helping Liberty study. The more encouraging Liberty was with the injured Mr. Knapp and his son, Samuel, the quicker Gerrett wished to leave the hospital.

Liberty had boundless energy, which rather exhausted him.

He tried to remain polite, but his mind drifted, until she gave a newly sewn shirt to Samuel. While Mr. Knapp wept as he shared how blessed his family had been, Gerrett stood awkwardly to the side and focused on one exchange.

I wish I could thank the person who paid my medical expense.

Sir, often people give for the blessing of giving and don't want thanks.

Liberty was that generous person!

Whatever exhaustion Gerrett had fled in that moment. Eventually, Liberty would face a train wreck of her life because of her own well-intended actions. Because of his own metaphorical "train wrecks," that was one collision he yearned to spare her.

He had to protect her.

Gerrett stepped forward and joined the conversation. After praying that Mrs. Knapp would find employment and that Mr. Knapp's leg would heal quickly, he silently led Liberty out of the hospital.

They stepped outside.

He immediately turned to her, raising her hood to cover her hair.

"If you give away what money you have," Gerrett said in a controlled voice to dampen his frustration, "you won't have the funds to stay in college."

Her face paled, which was surprising because the wind had grown stronger and more biting. Then her shoulders slumped.

"I know," she said dejectedly. "I enjoy giving to others. I don't think I can stop. It's who I am."

"You don't have to stop."

"I don't?"

"You *do* have to learn to be more discerning. Don't foolishly give away what you need to take care of yourself."

"More discerning!" she said, clearly aghast at his counsel. "I trust God to take care of my needs. I give and serve others out of my love for Him."

"But did you pray about paying for Mr. Knapp's medical expenses?"

She opened her mouth then closed it.

He took that as opportunity to continue. "You could have stolen the blessing God intended someone else to have in providing for the Knapps."

Her gaze shifted to the ground, looking almost pained. "That's not fair of you to say."

"Is it?"

Her gaze flew to his. "Do you pray about everything you do?"

"No, but I'm working at learning to pray more."

"Well, I didn't need to talk to God to know I didn't need the money—" her voice rose in volume "—and they did."

"Unless you intend on returning to Chicago and marrying some man your father has chosen, you need it. Until you establish your sewing business, you need it."

"God will provide," she said in *that* sort of tone. As if she had a faith greater than his.

"No matter how much faith we have," he said with a weakening damper on his frustration, "God doesn't always provide when we have a need. He doesn't always give us the desires of our heart. He doesn't always do what the Bible says He will do. Sometimes He just takes too long, so we have to take matters into our hands and do it ourselves. That's wrong and selfish."

Her eyes were watery, yet she smiled, albeit weakly. "I should go. The deportment rules—"

"It's getting dark. I'll walk you back."

"No! No," she repeated in a calmer voice. "I'll be fine. Please don't follow. Please?"

The hurt and brokenness he'd caused was there in her eyes. So unlike her. He wanted to say he was sorry. He wanted her to laugh and go back to being the joyful, optimistic, encouraging Liberty Judd that she was. He wanted to praise her charity, and be the man to help her and the one to light the joy in her eyes. But he couldn't be that for her. Ann was waiting for him.

Knowing he—knowing *they both*—needed time apart, Gerrett nodded. He had time to repair the rift between them.

She took several steps away then stopped. She looked at him over her shoulder, her eyes wide with sympathy. "I'm not going to cry." He must have given her a look to say, *Why are you telling me this?* because she added, "I thought you ought to know, so you don't feel bad thinking you broke my heart."

So laced with tenderness were her words, as if she wanted to comfort him, that he did. Feel comforted, that is.

He nodded again because that was the best he could manage considering the ache—the pounding—in his chest, and the tightness of the lump in his throat. *I'm sorry,* he wanted to say but couldn't.

She must have understood, because she nodded. Then she turned away.

He stood on the sidewalk in front of the hospital, watching her stroll down the snow-lined sidewalk and to the boardinghouse. Not until he saw her walk up the front steps did he turn around and walk the remaining distance to the Goswells' house. Tomorrow he would stay away from her.

His heart needed distance. He suspected hers did, too.

The next day, Gerrett accomplished his goal by staying in his room and working on his architectural designs from sunup to well past sundown. With forbearance and discipline of mind, a man could block out distractions. The underlying panic, joy and exhilaration he'd felt when around Liberty had also disappeared. He went to sleep rather proud of his accomplishment.

Liberty attended all her classes and took a French exam (A-minus) and another one in theology (less than A-minus but better than her previous D-plus).

On Tuesday, Gerrett worked on his drawings. He also spent time staring absently at his Bible, ignoring God's whispers, pondering his stupidity, thinking about Liberty, not eating, talking with Mrs. Goswell about Liberty, buying a ticket for Friday's first train out of Hillsdale, sending a telegram to his family about an engagement dinner Friday evening and pondering more of his stupidity.

Mostly, though, he thought about how he needed to stop thinking about Liberty.

Liberty attended classes and met with Lady Principal Whipple to discuss her relationship—which she denied—

with Gerrett. She also tried to find Katie, who still needed to have her gown hemmed for the Saint Valentine's Day Social. Instead, she finally met Joshua—a doctor, too!—who admitted he actually was Katie's arranged fiancé.

On Wednesday, Gerrett went sledding. Not by choice. Liberty went sledding. Also not by choice.

Chapter 13

Having done her best to overcome her chagrin at being volunteered by Ursula, who had been asked by Mrs. Goswell, to serve refreshments, Liberty handed the Reverend Scott a mug of hot cocoa. Being a native Floridian, he didn't take well to Michigan winters. Of all those out sledding, including the children, he was the most bundled. Poor man! She didn't fault him, though. Were it not for her fur-lined, hooded cloak, knitted scarf and gloves, she'd be more content to be inside by the fire. Although the fire she tended provided a decent amount of warmth to atone for being outside.

With the new snow that fell last night, causing another cancellation of Hillsdale classes, today called for living out one's inner child.

"She's going to make a wonderful mother," Liberty said to break the awkwardness between them since her rejection of his proposal.

The Reverend Scott held the mug with both gloved

hands, the rim inches from his lips as he blew on the steaming liquid. Behind his wire spectacles, his brown eyes blinked repeatedly. "Uhh, who w-w-w-will m-m-make a wonderf-f-ful mother?" he said between chatters of his teeth.

Liberty held back her smile and motioned with her head to the hill Samuel Knapp was climbing with Olive, who tugged their sleigh behind her. While she vowed to Olive that she wouldn't share her secret, after nursing her own broken heart, Liberty would see to it that Burton Scott moved past his affection for her and place his affections on a more suitable lady.

In particular—Olive.

"Miss W-W-Wittingham?" he said, his gaze in the same direction as Liberty's.

"Yes."

"She…uhhh…yes, she w-w-will."

"She is so lovely to look upon—don't you think? I think so," Liberty continued to say. "I will be surprised if she is not married by the summer. Hillsdale College has the finest men of character who are in need of wives. Come spring, I suspect Olive will be besieged with gentlemen callers. All of whom love Jesus as much as she does."

He looked to Liberty then back to the hillside where Olive and Samuel were waiting their turn to slide. His head slowly tilted, and his expression became that which he had last October when, after having disliked peaches all his twenty-four years, he realized they tasted delicious when added to sugar and baked in a cobbler. A realization he would have never made had he not trusted Liberty enough to take a bite of what she'd promised he'd like if he would just try it.

She hoped his trust would make his heart receptive to her words.

She eased beside him, her shoulder almost touching

his, her voice softening so only he could hear. "Yesterday, Miss Whipple told me to let go of *my* plans and discover what God's plan is for my life." She watched him through her peripheral vision. "I am praying, and I don't have all the answers yet, but I do know I'm not in God's plan for your life. I'm sorry. Maybe Olive is."

"Miss J-J-Judd," he said between shivers and teeth chatters, "your f-f-forthrightn-n-ness and g-g-graciousness are most appreciat-t-ted."

Seeing a group of college students approach, Liberty took a step to the side, increasing the distance between her and the man she hoped would fall in love with her friend. "Drink up, Mr. Scott. You need some internal warming."

While he sipped his cocoa, Liberty continued filling mugs from the kettle hanging over the fire. There had to be out sledding upwards of thirty children and near that number in adults, most of the latter college students. Including Professor Goswell. Except instead of Charmaine Finney, the woman with him was—

Her eyes widened. Miss Roper?

By the way Professor Goswell and Miss Roper laughed with each other, they looked happy.

"Gerrett was right," she muttered to no one in particular, and no one in particular paid heed to her words.

Then she shivered. Then she couldn't move. Not from the cool breeze nipping at her face, nor from the dusting of snowflakes falling from the nearby trees. Neither from her boots ankle-deep in the snow.

She couldn't move because she couldn't breathe. Literally. It made her dizzy, actually. But overjoyed. An overjoyed, dizzy, unable-to-breathe-or-move feeling, not at all how she'd ever felt before, especially after having spent seven years loving him and hearing her heart sing whenever he was near. Except—now, instead of hearing her heart's song, she heard nothing. The conversations around her and the laughter from those sledding, tossing snow-balls and enjoying refreshments all faded away.

Without looking around, without hearing his voice, even after how they'd parted on Sunday, she could feel his presence.

But he couldn't be here. He had drawings to finish. He had a soon-to-be fiancée waiting to be proposed to. And she couldn't *feel* him. People just didn't feel another's presence even when they couldn't see the other person. There had to be a logical explanation, such as— Well, the temperature *was* near freezing. She once read a study about winter-sports safety and how one's imagination was prone to run wild in extreme conditions.

Only this warmth spreading throughout her body didn't feel like frostbite or a hallucination. Perhaps madness.

Her toes tingled, which was from the snow covering the tips of her boots. Except the back of her neck tingled, too, and it was covered with her fur-lined hood, thus, no response to the wind or snow.

"What was I correct about?" his voice came from somewhere behind her.

Liberty gasped for air. She covered her chest with both hands as if someone had struck her. Then she looked over her shoulder.

Gerrett stood within an arm's-length distance from her, bundled in his greatcoat with a plaid scarf she recognized as belonging to Professor Goswell, with his gray derby cocked jauntily to the side, his left arm resting on the top of the wagon's sideboard. Based on the scruff on his face, she guessed he hadn't shaved in two days, maybe three. Still, he was here. She could grab him and never let go.

The Liberty Adele Judd she was wouldn't do any cleaving of the sort. Maybe if she were someone else. Maybe if she were impulsive. Maybe if she had the courage to stand up to her parents and tell them—respectfully, of course—that she would not allow them to control her life.

She whirled around to face him.

He smiled.

First in his eyes then on his lips, the very ones she remembered touching hers, the ones that gave her a kiss she shouldn't dream about but did. All that joy she'd felt moments earlier came rushing back, filling every inch of her skin. And she knew the truth.

What she *felt* was real.

She loved him. With every fiber, nerve, muscle and inch of her being. Even when he hurt her feelings. Even when he avoided her for almost three days.

She should want to grab him and never let go, yet instead, a wondrous peace filled her. She wanted him to be happy. She wanted him to be able to let go of his past and repair his relationship with his parents and grandparents by honoring them in fulfilling his family duty. She wanted him to love God foremost in his life. And she wanted him to follow God's plans for his life, even though that meant him walking—riding the train, actually—out of her life.

Her heart hurt, but it was a good hurt.

Gerrett motioned over his shoulder to the nearest sleigh. "Might I have a word with you?"

Without any warning, Liberty smiled. It was nothing more than a slight lifting of the corners of her mouth, but a smile nonetheless.

"Go on, Miss Judd," the Reverend Scott said. "I'll attend to the cocoa and the fire." While his tone had warmth, it no longer had the possessiveness Gerrett remembered from their first meeting.

She expressed her thanks then walked with Gerrett to where the horses stood.

He stopped. She stopped.

Gerrett sought her blue-gray eyes, and she boldly met his.

He blinked, taken aback. But when had Liberty ever hidden her thoughts or feelings? Her transparency was so…herself, which, under the circumstances, should have put him at ease. Instead, he felt even more uneasy. Shame did that to a man.

He took a deep breath.

She took one, too.

"I'm sorry," they said in unison.

She sputtered with laughter, and he felt the tension in the moment abate. He relished her joy. He thought of all sorts of amusing responses to make her laugh again, but now was not the time. He needed to apologize. No matter how humiliating it was.

She must have sensed it, too, because she regarded him dryly. "What's wrong?"

"Nothing—everything."

"I know." She sighed. "Gerrett, I don't mind discussing the weather until you feel comfortable with saying what you came here to say."

That was Liberty—candid yet gracious.

"The weather will attend to itself," he answered.

She looked relieved.

"Mrs. Goswell confiscated my drawings this morning. After a lengthy lecture about not avoiding our friends, she said I can only have them back after I spoke with you."

She clasped her hands in front of her. "Then I shall say nothing so you can speak quickly. You need to finish your work."

Gerrett swallowed to ease the tightness in his throat. "I chastised you about not seeking God's direction before you took care of Mr. Knapp's medical expense, yet I failed to seek God's direction if He wanted me to talk to you about it. Will you forgive me?"

She nodded, and he took that as a sign to continue.

"I'm a broken man. In the last year, my constant prayer has been 'Help me, Lord. I can't handle this.'" He waved at the space between them. "This—us—is a struggle for me because I'm not sure what I feel for you, and I don't want to enter marriage with Ann wondering if I am settling for second best."

"You said marrying her made good business sense."

"It does."

"Then why does it matter if she is first best or second?"

"Because—" Gerrett groaned. He wasn't used to someone, besides God, inviting him to be transparent. It hurt. It also felt freeing. "I always expected I would make a practical marriage, and then, like my parents and grandparents, I would fall in love with my spouse."

"That's ideal."

"What if this—" he waved again at the space between them "—is a stepping stone to love? What if this train wreck experience is something designed to take me to a deeper level of brokenness?"

Her gaze shifted to the sledders on the hillside. "I don't know. Maybe." She looked back at him. "How do you feel?" Strange that she didn't tack on *about me?*

"I feel sifted."

"How so?"

"God isn't letting me get by with things that He let me get by with before."

She nodded with understanding.

"When I ask Him why, He says He has a plan for my life. I don't know what that plan is," he said desperately. "I have things I need to make right by fulfilling my duty to my family. Instead, I'm here—with you—and God keeps sifting me."

She stepped forward and curled her gloved hand around his. "Is sifting such a bad thing?"

The hillside was full, dozens of people sledding, throwing snowballs and enjoying refreshments—some not but ten feet away—yet this spot near the horses felt utterly secluded. As if they were alone. As if no one could see them. Here she was gazing up at him, her eyes full of compassion, her hand gripping his, and then, somehow, she was closer. Or maybe he was. His lips, to be more specific, to hers. A dozen more inches and he could kiss her. He would. He wanted to.

He *yearned* to. He could tell she yearned for him to.

But she just stood there. Waiting.

He pondered that. Was she waiting for him to kiss her? No. For him to choose *not* to. Because he could tell—strange as it was—that she had already chosen not to. He straightened his shoulders, squared his jaw and took a cleansing breath. He was going to be all right. In the end. She would be, too.

"Goswell and I have a fencing match tomorrow after his last history class—your class."

"That's exciting news." The amusing twinkle in her eyes belied the sincerity of her actual words. Her sense of humor was so like his.

Gerrett restrained his smile. "It's an easy opportunity for extra credit."

"Mmm."

Mmm? What was he to take that to mean? "What do I have to offer to convince you to watch the match?" he asked. "Money? Gems? A puppy?"

She looked vaguely affronted. "Are you implying I'm bribable?"

"Everyone has a price. I'm hoping yours is furry."

"Since you asked, I have a list." She actually sounded serious. "First, come with me to the Saint Valentine's Day Social. Talk to Lady Principal Whipple long enough to convince her we are nothing but friends."

"Did she lecture you on the deportment rules and regulations?"

"It wasn't pleasant," she acknowledged with a crestfallen sigh. "Besides, I need to speak with George Quackenbush, and seeing you there is enough to keep him on proper behavior."

"Agreed."

She lowered her voice. "Second, sometime today I want you to mention to Burton Scott how pretty Olive Wittingham is."

Miss Wittingham was indeed a lovely young woman, so he didn't see how speaking the truth would be a problem for him.

He nodded. "Agreed."

"Don't agree too quickly. I'm not finished. Third, I want to name your firstborn. Even if it is a boy."

Gerrett blinked in surprise. "Seriously?"

She held her hands before her. "If that is too much for you, please know I am content with my C-minus in history."

He didn't grit his teeth like he wanted. By the time he had a firstborn, he doubted she'd remember his concession.

"All right, have it your way."

She stared gape-mouthed. "Seriously?"

He laughed. "You didn't think I'd agree?"

"No." Yet she was smiling. "Now I'm obligated to do the extra credit, aren't I?"

"Liberty!" came a distant voice.

Gerrett turned as she did to see Miss Wittingham running over to them, only without her young shadow. Liberty met her at the fire, where the Reverend Scott was still attending to the refreshments. He looked as concerned as Liberty.

"Olive, what's wrong?" she asked.

Miss Wittingham's face was flushed. "Nothing's wrong, silly," she said between breaths. "Mr. Goswell is organizing a sledding race. Five dollars split between the winners. Think of all the fabric you could buy after we win."

"Forget fabric! Two-fifty would pay for a month's stay at the boardinghouse."

They ran off, leaving Gerrett with Burton Scott.

"Miss Wittingham is a lovely woman." Gerrett intentionally kept his admiring gaze on the women while he casually remarked, "Is she courting anyone?"

"I thought you and Miss Judd...?"

"We're friends, nothing more. Shall we go watch the race?"

As they walked over to the talkative crowd teaming up, Gerrett noted that he didn't have to steer the good reverend to where Liberty and Miss Wittingham were standing. The younger man did it all on his own, and the woman Scott stood behind was Olive.

He leaned forward, rested his hand on Liberty's lower back and noted she stiffened. He whispered, "One of three terms complete."

Her lips pursed and gaze stayed focused ahead, yet she nodded, acknowledging him.

Gerrett moved his hand away and stepped back, putting a respectful distance between them. He could have said what he did without touching her. Should have. But he wanted one last physical connection with her.

Goswell whistled, and the crowd quieted.

"Adult teams must have one male, one female to make it fair." His gaze shifted around the crowd. "Teams line up at the bottom of the hill and race to the top. First team to reach the bottom with both sledders still on the sleigh wins."

Miss Wittingham turned to Liberty. "So much for us winning."

"I'll be your partner," Gerrett offered.

Miss Wittingham's hazel eyes shifted from Gerrett to Liberty then back to Gerrett. "You will?"

"No, he won't," Liberty interjected.

"I won't?"

She gave her head a shake. "I want to win, and how can I do that if *I* have no partner?" she said so innocently that even he almost believed her sudden competitiveness. "I'm sorry, Olive. With my business newly starting, I could use the winnings."

"I'll be your partner," the Reverend Scott blurted, looking at Miss Wittingham. "That is, if you don't mind."

"I don't mind," Olive answered with a pretty blush. Gerrett would be surprised if Scott hadn't fallen in love with her at that moment.

Liberty clapped her hands together. "Splendid! Now I don't feel so despicable for being selfish."

After Miss Wittingham and the Reverend Scott left to find a sled, Gerrett wrapped Liberty's arm around his before they went in search of their own sled. "If you're that desperate for a few dollars, then why didn't you ask me for it in exchange for your attending the fencing match?"

Her lips curved mischievously, and Gerrett realized *that* was all the answer he was going to receive.

He stopped at the remaining unclaimed sleigh. "Shall we?"

"Your excitement is contagious."

"Now that is a wheelbarrow full of sarcasm, Miss Judd."

"Do you *actually* want to sled and risk possible death?"

"Absolutely. Don't you?"

"Absolutely!"

Laughing, they lined up with the other teams.

Goswell whistled. And the race was on. A scramble

up the hillside and a streak down, sadly, did not result in their winning. Gerrett didn't mind. The day was a success.

And finally realizing one of the purposes for the emotional whirlwind he'd experienced in the past week, he returned to the Goswells' house. He reclaimed his vellum and spent the rest of the day and most of the night finishing his design for a house. For Liberty. And for her someday children to hide in.

Chapter 14

After her last class on Saint Valentine's Day, Liberty focused on the journal resting atop her lap and hastily wrote down the live-action lecture.

"Due to the evolution of firearms," Professor Goswell said between breaths and *clinks* of his rapier against Gerrett's, "the sword gradually became a weapon of secondary importance. The growth of the popularity of rapier as a civilian or dueling weapon marked the decline of the ancient, medieval European sword systems. However, the saber became popular as the military weapon of the European armies at the end of the last century."

"Especially during the Napoleonic wars," Gerrett added.

Liberty contained her grumbles. How long was this going to last? She had five pages of notes already! At this rate, her essay on the art of using the sword was going to be thesis-length.

Besides, it was almost noon, and her stomach was growling. Or at least it would be soon.

Sitting next to Miss Roper, Liberty continued to take notes. The men eased back and forth on their "line," while waxing eloquent on how sabers were used today by cavalries and infantries. Like Regency dandies, both wore white shirts, white waistcoats, tan breeches and knee-high boots, their agreed-upon attire. Their coats hung over the back of the Queen Anne chairs, which only added to her frustration.

Being in the same room with Gerrett was bothersome enough. Smelling his sandalwood-and-citrus cologne on his coat—

She gave in to her growl.

Miss Roper leaned toward Liberty, the fabric of her taffeta gown brushing against Liberty's calico dress. Much could be said complimentarily about Euphemia Roper— the least of which was her excellent taste in fashion.

"A classical fencer is supposed to be one who observes a fine position," Miss Roper whispered during a lull in Goswell's lecture. "See how both men keep form in attack and in defense?"

Nodding, Liberty jotted down *fencer observes fine position*.

"You aren't watching them."

"I need to see what I'm writing."

"So it is as I suspected."

As she suspected? Liberty met Miss Roper's green-eyed gaze. While not the classical golden beauty Charmaine Finney was, Miss Roper and her abundant chestnut hair could draw any man's attention. Her dark-lashed eyes tilted up ever so slightly at the edges.

"Mr. Divine and I aren't courting," Liberty explained, in not as assured a tone as she'd wanted it to be, "despite what you may believe. He is about to be engaged to a friend. I'm happy for him—for them."

Miss Roper shrugged, then straightened in her seat and watched the men, who were fencing furiously. "See how their attacks are fully developed? Their hits are marvelously accurate, both parries firm and ripostes executed with precision."

Parries and ripostes? Lost at what Miss Roper was talking about, Liberty looked to the men. She winced. Their weapons continually struck one another so quickly that she couldn't tell who was attacking and who defending.

Lord, keep Gerrett safe.

The moment she heard Miss Roper speak, she turned to her.

"This fluidity of movement of the fencer," Miss Roper instructed, her eyes taking on a glazed—almost enchanted—look, "is not possible unless his adversary is a party to it. Parries, attacks and returns, all rhyming together. He's magnificent...ehrm...I mean, they're magnificent to watch." She gasped suddenly.

Liberty whipped her head around to the men.

Gerrett lowered his foil and staggered backward as Professor Goswell swung his foil away from Gerrett's left arm. A streak of blood darkened the middle of Gerrett's shirtsleeve.

Despite the pinching from the cut on his arm, Gerrett smiled and drew several cleansing breaths. "Excellently done!" he said, slapping Goswell's back.

Liberty sat frozen on her chair.

Miss Roper grabbed the medicinal basket that Goswell's mother had insisted they bring. She hurried over to Gerrett, told him to hold the basket and immediately began attending to his wound.

Gerrett spoke low for only her to hear. "The cut is superficial."

She looked up from his arm. A tall woman, her gaze was almost leveled with his. She blinked, then her eyes widened as she realized what he was suggesting. She pressed the gauze firmly against his arm to stop the bleeding.

"Mr. Divine, I am sorry to say you will not bear a scar worth bragging about. Nor will you die, unless Ayden tainted his rapier with poison."

Goswell grinned. "I prefer not to kill off the few friends I have."

Gerrett watched the tension leave Liberty's face.

"My gratitude," he said for both Goswell's and Miss Roper's benefit. He handed his foil to Miss Roper and took over pressing the gauze against his arm. "I hear you are a skilled fencer. Why don't you resume the match in my stead?"

She gave a little curtsy. "You honor me, sir. However, I don't believe Ayden would enjoy being disarmed by me." She cast a taunting grin at Goswell. "Again."

To Gerrett's amazement, Goswell's face reddened.

"I, uhh…" he sputtered before resuming his normal dignified stance. "Seeing how I've already vanquished one foe today, I must focus on the purpose of this exercise." He stepped toward Liberty. "In fencing, as well as in most sciences, rules can only give general results. One cannot master the skill by reading a book or memorizing a list of rules."

Liberty held up the book he'd given her in class. "So I don't have to read Joseph Roland's *The Amateur of Fencing,* further known as—" she turned the front cover toward her and grimaced *"—A Treatise on the Art of Sword-Defence: Theoretically and Experimentally Explained Upon New Principles; Designed Chiefly for Per-*

sons who Have Only Acquired a Superficial Knowledge of the Subject."

How she managed that without adding a single *blah,* Gerrett would never know. She continually impressed him.

Goswell laughed. "Actually, yes, you still have to read it if you wish to pass my class." He offered the hilt of his foil. "Here."

Liberty looked at him as if he'd grown seven crowned heads and ten horns. "Why?"

"To master fencing, one must also practice."

"Uhh, no."

"Please, Miss Judd," Miss Roper cajoled. "During the colonial era, women participated in fencing clubs here in America. It is an acceptable sport for females."

"I am not dressed appropriately to fence."

"Neither am I."

Liberty placed her book back under her closed journal. Gerrett assumed she was debating how she could flee the room without being conscripted. Thus, he stepped around Miss Roper, walked past Goswell and sat in the chair next to Liberty.

"Amazing to me how you were willing to risk death sledding down a hill yet won't risk a little cut, at most, learning the basics of fencing."

She glared at him. "Are you implying I am a coward?"

He shrugged.

She growled under her breath in a manner he was growing quite accustom. In fact, it made him want to kiss her. Then again, the wanting to kiss her was a constant feeling. He grabbed the edges of her books and, after a few tugs against her resistance, took them from her.

He nodded toward Miss Roper. "Take a risk. You may have fun."

"Because I enjoy being slashed to death."

"Again, more sarcasm."

He stared at her. She stared at him.

Then with a loud sigh, she stood and took the rapier from Goswell. "What do I do?"

Gerrett sat quietly as Goswell and Miss Roper explained the basics of being on guard and how to keep one's eyes on her adversary's sword, not eyes, in order to observe the motion of his wrist.

"Put your right foot forward," Goswell said, "and back foot at a ninety-degree angle with your front foot."

"Now bend your knees like this," Miss Roper said, demonstrating. "This is how you start *en garde*."

"You will go back and forth this imaginary line—" Goswell motioned to the ground "—with a series of steps called advances and retreats. Mia, show her the footwork."

After several minutes explaining what Miss Roper demonstrated, Goswell left the ladies to their imaginary line. He sat next to Gerrett.

"Did Miss Roper really disarm you?" Gerrett asked, while his new friend continued to watch the women.

His cheek twitched. "In more ways than one."

Gerrett nodded, understanding exactly what Goswell meant. He raised the gauze on his arm to see that the bleeding had stopped. After noticing what was in the medicinal basket, he found a jar of ointment, unscrewed the cap and rubbed the salve onto his surface cut before returning the jar to the basket. He turned his attention to Miss Roper teaching Liberty a simple pattern of parries and ripostes.

"Now," Miss Roper said, "let's repeat that pattern. Engage." She thrust her rapier to third position.

Liberty blocked it. "When does the fun start?" she asked then blocked to the left this time.

"Now," Miss Roper answered as they continued the pattern.

"My arm is hurting."

"Excellent." She sounded just like Goswell. "Now let's increase the speed of our movements."

Liberty groaned yet continued following Miss Roper's instruction, until— "Oww!" She lowered her weapon and looked at her arm.

Gerrett leaned forward, resting his elbows on his knees, his pulse increasing. He couldn't see a cut in Liberty's sleeve. In fact, it looked like Miss Roper had only tapped her with the side of her round blade, not the sharp tip.

Miss Roper lowered her weapon, too. "My apologies. However, you will see there is no wound. This time, instead of only defending against my attack, I want you to surprise me." She raised her rapier. "Engage."

Liberty cast a scowl at Goswell then at Gerrett. She resumed the pattern of movements Miss Roper had taught her. Never once did she do anything surprising. After each set, Miss Roper increased the speed, hitting Liberty's arm and skirt several times.

Liberty finally threw her rapier to the ground. "Why are you doing this?" she yelled, flushed and breathing hard.

"Because you won't go on the offense!"

"I don't want to!"

"Thus, you quit?"

"No, Mia, I'm walking away."

"Then you are a coward."

"Because I think fencing is pointless?"

"Because you're selfish! All you care about is your classes and this school." Miss Roper stepped forward. "You won't fight for love, just like Ayden—" Stricken, she covered her mouth, her face paling. "Oh, Liberty, I'm so sorry. That was uncalled for. I didn't mean—"

"It's all right," Liberty said softly. She smoothed back

the red-gold hair that had loosened from her chignon. She took another deep breath. "It's— I should— Umm, I need to go help Ursula."

Gerrett stood. "I'll go with—"

"No." She walked to him and grabbed her book and journal. "I need to be sifted. Alone."

Once he nodded, she left the room without a goodbye to any of them.

"Before you say anything," Gerrett said to Miss Roper, who was in tears, "please know Liberty doesn't hold grudges. She'll be fine tomorrow."

Goswell took a step toward Miss Roper.

"Don't." Instead of saying more, she fled the parlor.

Gerrett sank back in his chair.

Goswell sat in his, too, resting his head back against it, his gaze on the ceiling. "What do you advise we do now?"

"First, we put the room back in order," Gerrett said quietly as he stared at the rapier Liberty had tossed to the ground. He sensed whatever turmoil raging inside her wasn't centered on her feelings for him. God was doing sifting of His own in her.

Work Your will in her, Jesus.

Slapping his thighs, he looked to Goswell. "Then we clean up for the Saint Valentine's Day Social."

Shifting his head just enough for his gaze to meet Gerrett's, Goswell said, "Do you think Liberty and Mia will attend after what happened?"

"They're women," Gerrett said with assurance. "They simply can't *not* go to a party."

Chapter 15

Approximately three hours later, Gerrett and Ayden attended the social. The ever kind and ever delightful Miss Charmaine Finney, to their chagrin, made sure they spoke to everyone in attendance.

Which never included Liberty or Miss Roper.

By 5:04 p.m., Gerrett walked with Ayden back to the Goswell house after having drunk too much lemonade and eaten too many cookies, and gained George Quackenbush's agreement that the man would cease pursuing Liberty. With a most valiant effort, he tried convincing Lady Principal Whipple that he wasn't in love with the very woman he came to the social to see. In response, Miss Whipple drew him to the side of the room and gave him a lecture the likes of which he hadn't heard since he sank his father's sailboat in Lake Michigan.

After reaching the Goswell house, Gerrett pondered more on Miss Whipple's advice—*Let go of your plans*

*and desires, Mr. Divine, and discover what God's plans
are for your life. Liberty must do the same.*

That was why, instead of seeking Liberty at the boardinghouse, he sought Scripture, spent time in prayer and
pursued Mr. and Mrs. Goswell's wise counsel. The most
considerate thing he could do for Liberty was to walk out
of her life as quickly as he had entered.

In the morning, he would return to Chicago and begin
falling in love with the woman he was going to marry.

As she waited for the bread Ursula had made to finish baking, Liberty sat at the kitchen's small table. Today
hadn't been the most enjoyable Saint Valentine's Day, but
it had been an emotional one, nevertheless. After having spent an hour on her bed crying, praying and taking
inventory of her life following her fencing match with
Miss Roper, she had decided to forgo fun in lieu of responsibility.

While her fellow students had attended the social, she'd
studied for her Latin and history exams, finished her as-
signments in French, literature and theology, and began
writing the rough draft of her extra-credit history essay,
which was now complete. Once she finished finding a
few additional quotes to add, she'd write her final version. In her best handwriting. In pen, even! That alone
would take several hours, but Liberty was determined to
give it the same due diligence as she'd put into sewing a
gown or doing an alteration.

She was an adult and needed to act like one.

Adults didn't depend on extra credit to help them pass
a class. Adults weren't content with a C-minus.

She adjusted the flame in the oil lamp. What she'd give
for more than nine hours of daylight! Once satisfied with
the height of the flame, she began reading the last chapter

in *The Amateur of Fencing.* Study notes, textbooks and pencils covered the table.

"I have never seen you work so meticulously on an essay," Ursula said as she cleaned the kitchen following the evening meal. "From where comes this new dedication to studying?"

Liberty looked up from her book and frowned.

Ursula stopped wiping the counter. "*Libelle,* did you hear what I asked?"

"Oh. I heard you. It's just—" With a sigh, she inserted a bookmark to hold her place. "I'm a coward, Ursula. Or, I have been."

"Why do you think this?"

"Because I would rather give minimal effort and be satisfied with good enough to succeed, than go all out and risk failing miserably."

"Quite insightful."

Insightful and not altogether pleasant.

Liberty held her book against her chest. "What Miss Roper said to me earlier today hurt. I don't want to be disappointed or lose or have my heart broken again. After Gerrett broke my heart five years ago, I've never risked anything. When I'm faced with a foe who I think can't be defeated, I run and hide. Attending Hillsdale to escape my parents is the perfect example. But I'm not going to be that Liberty Judd anymore."

Ursula leaned against the counter and nodded thoughtfully. "Will you say this to your father when he arrives? Demand your right to live your life on your own terms?"

Liberty's chest ached. The problem with being sifted by God was that He exposed flaws that one would rather keep hidden. Admitting she was a coward was far easier than admitting—

"I've also been a sanctimonious prig."

Ursula straightened in obvious offense to Liberty's self-incrimination. "Not you."

"Yes, me." Liberty's throat tightened. "I call myself a Christian, yet how have I behaved toward my parents? 'Your sins are great. Mine are forgiven.'"

Ursula blinked, her eyes watery. She didn't have to speak for Liberty to know her surrogate mother realized she perceived herself correctly.

"I haven't loved or honored them," she continued. "I haven't shown them any of the grace that God has given me. Why would they want to have anything to do with Jesus, when I don't show them a Jesus worth getting to know?"

"What do you do now?"

"I am going to finish this essay."

Ursula looked confused.

"My father doesn't need to come to Hillsdale. I need to go to him. After my Friday classes are over, I'm returning to Chicago."

"To stay?"

Liberty shrugged. She had no idea what her future held. What mattered was that she was going to try to make things work with her parents.

"To talk. I need to apologize for my rebellious and pious attitude," she admitted, feeling the pinch of shame rising to chastise her again.

Only she wouldn't listen.

She wouldn't let shame stop her from atoning.

Liberty shifted on the chair. "I'm going to cooperate with my parents in finding me a husband, but I will ask if they would first allow me to finish my classes this quarter at Hillsdale."

Ursula nodded thoughtfully again. "They may not agree."

"I'm all right with that, too."

Her future had never been more uncertain, yet neither had she ever felt such peace.

Liberty placed her book atop her notes. "There is a verse in First John that says, 'let us not love in word, neither in tongue; but in deed and in truth.' To love and honor my parents, I should begin with serving them. I've never done that." She smiled. "This will be an interesting adventure."

"You give them opportunity to take advantage of you."

She nipped at her bottom lip. How many times since the fencing match had she besieged that argument with God? Knowing full well her parents would likely do so. Knowing her parents weren't good people. Knowing her father would try to break her spirit as he had killed Leonidas's and Lurana's.

Freely you have received, freely give.

That made no sense. Why empower her father's desire to control by agreeing to an arranged marriage? Why willfully let him take advantage of her? Why give freely to anyone who asked it of her? There was no logic in that. None.

In fact, doing so was foolish. Ludicrous, even!

The deeper issue, though, was why serve a God who asked His followers to *"give to everyone who asks of you, and from him who takes away your goods do not ask them back"*? It was as if Jesus wanted His followers to give without expecting anything in return. Give knowing full well you were going to be taken advantage of. That went against the very grain of humanity.

Nowhere in Scripture could she find where God seemed concerned about people taking advantage of Him. And people did. When they wasted the talents, skills, time, life, wealth, resources and imagination He had given them, yet Jesus continued to give sunlight to the evil and the good, summer rain to the just and unjust. The paradox of it all was what the Reverend Dunn had been teaching this semester in her theology class.

And she *finally* understood!

Maybe instead of caring about not being taken advantage of, she ought to offer her life as a living sacrifice for God to use for His glory. Then allow God to work things out for her good. That had to be real faith. Real love.

She met Ursula's intent gaze.

"God has been sifting me," she explained in a voice so tight she could barely speak. "I want to love others as Jesus loves, and I now realize to love as He does means I have to begin with the hardest people for me to love—my parents."

With a sigh, Ursula walked over to the table. She sat next to Liberty, taking Liberty's hands in her own. "What about Mr. Divine?"

"Sometimes I feel as if my heart is going to explode from my chest because it can't contain the love I have for him."

A tear began to roll down her cheek; she wasn't sure how it was possible, considering how many tears she'd shed after the fencing match. She fought the lump in her throat. Why couldn't a heart's healing be less painful?

Ursula touched Liberty's cheek. *"Mein liebes kind."*

Before she knew it, she was in Ursula's arms, weeping. She had not cried for Gerrett since seeing him climb out of the tipped train car. Nor did she now.

For the past seven years and three months and ten days, she had lived with hope that maybe they would be together someday. That maybe he would love her. She cried for the hope that was dying and because of the fear growing, twisting and withering inside. She wanted more than an arranged marriage. She wanted to experience euphoric love and rapturous desire with someone who felt the same. She wanted to feel again that nervous, excited tingle from knowing the man she loved was near, even though she couldn't see him.

Then she cried for hiding and running, and because she accepted what she had to be. And because in the deepest recesses of her heart, where she kept her hopes and dreams, she feared—was scared spitless—she'd never experience a love like this again. Illogical yet, well, there it was.

Her chest ached. Her face hurt. Her eyes burned.

Liberty breathed deep, trying to regain control. "I'm all right," she whispered.

"I need to see to the bread," Ursula said, pulling gently away.

"And I need to finish reading this book." Liberty wiped the last of the tears from her eyes. "How about some coffee? I have a long night of schoolwork ahead of me."

"Miss Judd, is there a problem with your ticket to Chicago?"

"No, Mr. Smith," Liberty said over the guttural whistles and rumblings of the approaching train.

The depot's warning bell began to ring.

Bundled in her green velvet cloak over the apple-green, five-flounced silk gown she'd made and saved for a special occasion, she laid payment on the counter in the telegraph office and rested her portmanteau on the ground. Gerrett had left Hillsdale on the first train out, without saying goodbye.

Her heart tightened at the thought of him.

No sense taking offense to his action. Goodbyes were never enjoyable. *Jesus, keep him safe as he takes his next journey.*

As the train's *whooh-whoohs* grew in volume, the clicky-clack rattle of the tracks increased.

She untied her right glove then pulled it off one finger

at a time. "As I was waiting for the noon train to arrive, I realized I needed to send a telegram."

As he stood behind the counter, the enigma named Homer Smith raised his spectacles from his nose to the top of his head—sunshiny blond and unoiled today, she noted. He wasn't strikingly handsome, yet he was quite pleasant to look at. Even with the horizontal scar on his left cheek that had to have come from…a fencing wound! From a duel? From war? In fleeing a—

"Miss Judd?"

"Yes?"

His blue-green eyes focused on her. "The train is almost here. To who do ye…ehrm…you wish to send the telegram?" That had to have been an Irish or maybe Scottish lilt in his speech.

"My brother," she absently answered.

Liberty glanced over her shoulder to be sure they were still alone in the telegraph office, although through the windows she could see the platform was steadily filling with travelers preparing to board. The train's brakes hissed and screeched as it approached the station.

Liberty turned back to Mr. Smith and lowered her voice. "I don't need to know why you are hiding or from who, but please know you have friends here in Hillsdale."

His Adam's apple bobbed. "Thank you. Fill out the paper," he said briskly, "and I'll—"

At the sound of the telegraph beeping, Mr. Smith began transcribing. Liberty quickly wrote out her message. The telegraph beeps stopped. She handed payment and the paper to Mr. Smith, who stared absently at it. The engine of the westbound train eased past the depot, brakes squealing to a halt.

"Is there a problem?" she asked, her heartbeat increasing.

He laid her message down. After stretching to see out

the depot window, he dug through the bag she'd never seen him without. He withdrew a leather-bound scroll.

"Mr. Divine asked me to deliver this to you at the boardinghouse once I finished work."

Liberty took it from him, untied the string and unrolled the scroll to see sheets of vellum. A piece of stationary fell to the ground, and she gasped in awe at the intricate drawings. "His replacement designs."

"'For you and your someday children to play hide-and-seek.'" He gave her a sheepish look. "That's what he wrote on the stationery. I couldn't help peeking inside the scroll."

And now Gerrett had nothing to give Ann Bartlett as an engagement gift. Fondness didn't cause a man to do this. Kindly affection didn't, either.

Gerrett Divine had fallen in love with her.

Her heart leaped. Then stumbled and fell.

Even if he did love her, he would do his duty. She would, too. Knowing that, she refused to grow maudlin. Her grades at Hillsdale were improving. After much prayer, she'd given one of her sewing machines to Samuel Knapp's mother and posted an advertisement recommending Mrs. Knapp's business. And she had a peace about how to make things right with her parents, which Lady Principal Whipple had agreed was a wise course of action before she granted permission to travel to Chicago for the weekend.

Liberty tucked the note in with the vellum drawings and rewrapped them with the leather cover. She placed the scroll inside her portmanteau.

"Mr. Smith, if you could see to the telegram, I will be most appreciative." Pulling her glove back on, Liberty took a step from the counter.

"May the hill rise behind you, Miss Judd, and may the mountain be always over the crest—" his voice broke

"—and may the God that ye believe in hold ye in the palm of his hand."

After whispered thanks, she stepped into the wintry breeze, easing through the platform where the westbound train to Chicago was being boarded. One week later and she was returning to the very city she'd sworn she'd never step foot in again.

All because of a train wreck.

Chapter 16

Liberty adjusted her skirts on the carriage bench, thrilled to be out of the blustery wind. The five-minute walk from the train station to the carriage left her face feeling chapped.

As Leonidas took his seat in the carriage opposite her, she eased her portmanteau against her hip. Not that she distrusted her brother. Merely, she couldn't let him discover what was inside. Not for her sake, but for Gerrett's. Mostly for precious Ann Bartlett, who didn't need to know what the man she was about to be engaged to had given another woman.

"So if our parents aren't home," she asked, "then where are they?"

Leonidas smiled in a manner that reminded her of the times during her childhood when he'd promise all would be well *and then* allowed her to take the punishment when they were caught misbehaving. Were it not for the six years' difference in their ages, with their coloring and facial similarities, they could be twins.

He would have no shame in saying he was the good twin, of course.

Liberty couldn't help rolling her eyes. She also knew him well enough to know his smile meant something more than a smile. "What are you scheming this time, brother dear?"

"Merely escorting my favorite sister to supper at the Tremont," Leonidas said with a familiar charm.

He removed his top hat and tossed it along with his gloves onto the bench. He straightened the front of his gray overcoat then knocked on the ceiling with his cane, signaling the driver it was time to leave. The carriage jolted into motion.

Liberty watched him suspiciously.

From the moment he'd met her when she disembarked the train, she hadn't smelled liquor on his breath—a first in the past year. Nor did she feel a flask inside his coat pocket when they shared a lengthy hug. His drinking aside, she loved him. His predilection for getting her in trouble—

She couldn't fight her smile, because despite his flaws, she adored him.

He cocked his head, regarding her. "You look different."

"Seems fitting after what I experienced this last week."

"Ahh."

"Ahh?"

His gaze shifted to the glass window nearest him, to the orange-and-blue sky as the sun set. Gone was the delightful rake, replaced with the grieving widower. She'd prayed with him, prayed for him and defended him against those who blamed him for his wife's death. She couldn't help him if he wouldn't accept her help. Wouldn't even admit he needed it.

By the number of turns the carriage took and the lengthy time that passed in silence, they had to be nearing the Tremont House.

Leonidas turned back to her.

His smile grew lopsided, jaunty. "I take it you saw Gerrett."

"I did." No sense denying it. "I take it you spoke to him."

"Gave him a ride from the depot earlier today, like I'm doing for you."

"You are a good friend," she said sincerely, "and a good brother."

He coughed. That he was uncomfortable with the compliment she saw with clarity. Not that he'd never been praised, for she knew he had. But praise for being charming or handsome wasn't the same as being applauded for chivalry and good manners.

"Libby, is he in love with you?"

I hope not since he's marrying Ann. She fingered a button on her cloak, her pulse increasing. "I take it he told you of his time in Hillsdale?"

"Yes, but he said nothing of you." Leonidas leaned forward, resting his elbows on his knees. "He looked different from the Gerrett I saw two months ago in Marseille."

"You find that suspicious, why?"

"In France he was accepting of his family's request that he marry Ann."

Liberty didn't respond. She didn't want to discuss Gerrett with her brother.

Leonidas watched her with rapt attention. "When I met him at the station this morning, he looked like he carried Atlas's burden. Hillsdale isn't a large village. I would wager that my little sister sought out the man she's loved since she was fifteen. Not to mention her compassionate heart would go out to a man injured in a train collision."

"Men don't fall in love with compassionate hearts."

"But this—" he waved in the air in front of her "—alone is enough to attract him. Did you pray with him? Did you talk about God? Because that itself is enough to entice him. Did you do any of the things that cause men to be besotted with you?"

"You make me sound like a nun-turned-seductress."

"What you are is encouragement, sunshine and honesty bundled in one irresistible picture."

She released a nervous laugh. "That's how you condense my virtues?"

"I'm your brother. Praising you goes against my nature."

She gave him a little smirk. "You may cease extolling my virtues. I'd hate for you to suffer on my behalf. *And* I didn't seek Gerrett out."

His eyes widened. "No?"

"No." Gerrett had sought her out, but Leonidas didn't need to know that. Then she smiled because she was rather proud of her unaffectedness in response to his questioning. But mostly because she knew a smirk would annoy him as payback for his, for all practical purposes, nun-turned-seductress slight.

The carriage stopped.

Leonidas straightened. "Why are you protecting him?"

Liberty lost what little amusement she had.

The carriage door opened, letting in a chilly breeze, but neither she nor Leonidas collected their things. Or moved to the open door.

"Leo, Gerrett has a future that doesn't include me, and I am accepting of that. I want him and Ann to be happy."

"What if I don't?"

Before she could question him, he climbed out of the carriage.

Liberty followed, gripping her portmanteau in her left hand and claiming her brother's arm with her right. Dinner at the Tremont. She could manage this. At least meeting in a public place lessened the chances of their parents behaving untowardly.

Leonidas escorted her through the opulent foyer. They left their winter garb and her portmanteau with the concierge.

As they walked across the marble floor, she stared in awe at the interior architecture like she always did when at the Tremont. The five-story hotel boasted majestic lobbies, monumental staircases, elegant parlors, cafés, a barber shop, bridal suites, dining rooms, ballrooms, promenades, hundreds of private bedrooms and baths and the latest luxuries, such as steam heat, gas lighting, elevators and French chefs. No wonder Ann Bartlett lived here. Doing so was a convenient way to set up a trouble-free, elegant household.

Leonidas's arm tensed under her fingers, drawing her attention to him.

What if I don't? he'd said.

What had he meant by that? He didn't want Gerrett to be happy. He didn't want Ann to be happy. Or—

Gasping, Liberty looked at her brother's handsome yet stony profile. His wife's death was over a year ago. Perhaps he didn't want Gerrett and Ann to be happy *together*.

"Leo, are you in love with Ann?" she asked as she practically ran to keep up with his sudden brisk pace.

"Yes."

"Does she know?"

"No."

"Then say something to her."

"If I tried to steal Ann from Gerrett—" His voice

choked, weakened. "He and Ann are the only friends I have. I can't lose either of them."

His fear ripped at her heart.

"Libby, if you love Gerrett, stop the engagement. For me."

Leaving her no time to answer, he maneuvered her into the dim gas-lit dining hall, filled with people sitting at white-skirted tables that surrounded the dance floor.

"Good evening, Mr. Judd," the maître d' called out. "Your parents are at your usual table. I explained to Mr. Edward Judd that all the private rooms were booked. He kept offering a higher price and demanding we find a room. We are trying, but our other paying guests—"

"Say no more, Mr. Aurand." Leonidas paused walking long enough to respond. "Stop looking. Sitting with the unwashed masses will be good for him."

Liberty tried to school her features, but how could she dampen the shock she felt. Her brother took meals at the Tremont enough times to have a *usual* table. Had he spent his meals alone, or with Ann?

Leonidas wove them around several filled tables to a round one near the back of the rectangular room. Close enough to the dance floor to have easy access, yet far enough from the orchestra to have a conversation without yelling or having to lean close to another person to be heard.

Father sat puffing his cigar and giving an angry glare at what was probably a stock report he held in his other hand. Work never waited. Her stepmother, Caroline, talked with the man sitting on her left. Monsieur Claude de Framboise was the premier gown designer in Chicago and a "fill-in" escort when Father wasn't available to attend his second wife's myriad social functions. The peacock-blue silk gown Caroline wore clearly showcased de Framboise's newest obsession—low-necked bodices and triple-tiered skirts with scalloped edges.

The seamstress in Liberty was reluctantly impressed, considering how much she disliked the pompous man.

"Are we late?" Leonidas said in that chipper tone of his.

Caroline's face paled.

Monsieur de Framboise stood, gave a down-the-nose glance at the dark green fringe on Liberty's silk gown's short sleeves, as well as each of the five flounces, then excused himself. *Fringe,* she'd once heard de Framboise say, *should be left in the last decade.*

Father sucked in a long, angry breath through his nose. "Yes, you are late," he barked, tossing the report onto the table. "As usual. Have they cleared us a private room yet?"

Liberty felt the muscles in her brother's arm tighten. "Any minute now it'll be available. They asked that we patiently wait here in the meantime."

Father turned his steely gaze upon her. "I see you elected to finally honor my wishes and return to your proper place."

Liberty felt her hackles rise. He wasn't the enemy, though. Love was patient and kind and kept no record of wrongs.

"Father, you're looking well." She stepped forward and kissed his cheek then her stepmother's. "You, too, Caroline."

Leonidas pulled out the seat for her to sit. And thus began their first family dinner since Christmas.

The curtains from the private dining room to the dining hall parted, and the hotel waitstaff entered, bringing in the dessert. Gerrett hadn't eaten any of the earlier courses, so he doubted this one would appeal to him any more than the others had.

This course, though, ended with his official marriage proposal.

He sat at the head of the table, with Ann to his right, then his mother next to her. His father sat at the other end. On the other side of the table were Grand-mère and Grandfather. He should feel at home. After all, he was surrounded with love.

His mother and grand-mère complimented Ann on her pearl-decorated pink gown and how it accented the blackness of her hair. Grandfather and Father discussed the expected completion date for the new passenger station being built for the use of the Illinois Central, Michigan Central and Burlington railroads.

Gerrett stared absently at the plate before him.

The only engagement gift he had to offer Ann was an emerald ring his mother had given him. *So you at least have something,* she'd said upon his arrival back to the house that afternoon following an unsuccessful trip to the jewelers, where every gem made him think of Liberty.

His mother's ring burned a hole in his coat pocket.

"Parlez-vous anglais?" Ann whispered, leaning to the edge of the table. Her brown eyes glinted with amusement.

"My apologies." He picked up his fork and forced a smile. "How is your meal?"

"Gerrett, we've known each other since you were in knickers and I was pretending to be a boy so I could wear them, too. You can be honest. Are you having second thoughts?"

He took a bite of crème brûlée to keep from answering.

She touched his hand, stilling him from scooping another spoonful. "Do you want to marry me?"

"You will make a superb wife," he said without pause.

"I do not accept that as an answer to my question."

"Your question?" Grandfather interjected. For an eighty-three-year-old man, Gerrett Henry Divine II had exceptional hearing, when it benefitted him. "Mrs. Bartlett, did you propose to my grandson?"

Ann smiled beautifully. "Grandfather Divine, I asked Gerrett if he *wanted* to marry me, not if he *would*."

The room fell silent.

Every eye turned to Gerrett.

Father motioned to the waitstaff, and they emptied the room. He then leaned forward in his seat. "Well? Do you want to marry her? Or is she an obligation to you?"

Gerrett looked from his parents to his grandparents. At this moment, with how queasy his nerves made him feel, he was glad he hadn't eaten much of anything.

Liberty twisted her spoon in her hand, torn between enduring the tomato bisque and placating her palate. Father was the only Judd who liked tomato bisque, and because he always ordered everyone's meals, that's what they ate. No one *ever* contradicted him.

She had to speak. Or forever hold her peace.

She looked to her father and stepmother. "I am sorry I've been a disappointment to you both."

They both watched her intently—Father with a clenched jaw, Caroline nervously twisting the dropped V of her diamond necklace.

Leonidas withdrew his pocket watch and rested it on the table between them.

Liberty debated questioning his action and where it was he had to go to following the dinner, but she knew her brother. Since his wife's suicide, he shared little of his life with anyone.

Since no one spoke, she figured she ought to continue. Not that she wanted to. If she had a choice, she would avoid the conversation entirely, flee back to Hillsdale and begin living on her own without her parents' interference.

But that was cowardly. Plus Father would know where to find her. She would have to flee to an island in the Pacific.

Her heart was pounding, lungs grasping for air, and her legs shook with the need to escape. Still, she said—

"I am also sorry for my rebellious attitude, for fleeing Caroline's birthday ball last Friday, for refusing to consider any suitors you've ever chosen for me and for not responding to your numerous telegrams. None of those behaviors has been honoring or respectful."

Her parents both nodded their heads.

Leonidas stopped pretending to eat his soup and stared, eyes wide.

She placed her spoon on the table. "Instead of being in conflict, I would like us to work together."

"What are you offering?" Father asked.

"A slight amendment to our original agreement." Liberty fingered the fringe on her skirt's top flounce. Her chest felt as if a grip was constricting all the air, yet she'd come too far to stop now. "I finish this quarter's classes at Hillsdale. Then I return to Chicago. I would like to find a man here who shares my faith and bring him to you for approval."

Father's dark brows drew down over his eyes.

Caroline looked to him for a response.

"Eat your soup," Father demanded. "I'm paying good money for it."

Caroline immediately obeyed.

Leonidas picked up his spoon.

Liberty didn't.

Her brother kicked her under the table then gave her a for-your-own-self-preservation-eat glare.

Every nerve in her body tense, Liberty looked from her brother to the soup that represented another aspect of her life her father insisted on controlling. She wasn't soup. She was an adult. Not even a court of law would hold her parents responsible for her actions. How did she balance respecting her father when he showed none to her?

With love.

Could she? What if it wasn't enough?

Give freely.

Liberty closed her eyes. *I don't know if I'm able.*

Try.

She released the breath she'd been holding. Then she picked up her spoon and drew upon all the courage, love and grace she had.

"Father," she said tenderly, "do you ever remember your parents demanding you eat something you didn't like?"

A muscle at his jaw flinched.

She presumed that meant yes.

His eyes then shifted from her face to her tomato bisque. Liberty looked down to her right hand poised over her bowl, clenching the spoon and trembling.

"Why are you shaking?" Father asked, his voice as gentle as it used to be during her childhood when she had fond—not fearful—memories of him. When she actually felt like he loved her. Her mother's death had turned him into such a cold man. Into a man who used his anger, authority and words as weapons.

"I am afraid of you."

He winced as if she'd struck him.

She winced, too, because she was sorry for being honest, and even sorrier that she feared him.

"I don't like tomato bisque." And that earned another swift kick from her brother and a gasp from Caroline.

"You never said anything," Father grumbled.

"You never asked," Liberty countered with tenderness. "I will eat it because you ordered it. I want to enjoy meals together. However, if you continue to order for me without asking what I would like, then I will eat alone.

Please show me the same respect and consideration that you ask of me."

"Liberty Adele Judd, what has come over you?" Caroline glared at her. "You will not dishonor your father."

"Yet *you* do," Father quipped, "with that dressmaker."

"I've never—" Caroline covered her mouth with her napkin to stifle her cry.

"Apologize," Leonidas seethed. His body did not move in the chair, yet the air around him coiled with tension that Liberty could feel. If he gripped the spoon any tighter, she'd swear he'd break it in half.

"Son, people are watching," Father warned. "You need to simmer down."

"And *that* is what happened after the trains collided."

Gerrett resumed eating his crème brûlée as his parents, grandparents and Ann sat quietly, each processing what he had shared about (1) meeting Liberty, (2) his apologizing for breaking her heart five years ago and how they became friends, (3) his house designs being stolen, (4) his feelings for Ann, (5) the shifting God had done in him, (6) what Lady Principal Whipple had advised him, (7) how he realized that he didn't want to leave architecture and take over the company and (8) if anyone should take over managing Divine investments, Ann should do it.

He had glossed over his time with and attraction to Liberty. He couldn't let Ann think that he was in love with another woman.

Father and Grandfather kept slowly nodding their heads. Of the three women in the private dining room, Ann seemed to take the news with the least amount of shock. Her face had no expression; she seemed accepting of what he'd shared. His mother and grand-mère stared wide-eyed.

Gerrett put his spoon down and pulled out the emerald ring his mother had given him. He stood. "Mrs. Ann Bartlett, would you do me the honor—"

Ann bolted to her feet. "I think I would like to dance."

Gerrett looked to his parents and grandparents.

"Go on," Father said. "None of us are ready for a proposal."

"Of course." After pocketing the ring, Gerrett draped Ann's arm around his and strode to the curtain partition separating the private room from the rest of the dining hall. Gerrett parted the velvet cloth. "After you."

Ann stepped through then immediately spun around, all the color draining from her face. "I've changed my mind," she said, pushing at him, yet he didn't move.

A sudden shattering of glass caused the attention of those in the hall to momentarily shift to the left side of the room. The orchestra never skipped a beat. The other hotel guests returned to their business.

"Please," Ann begged, "let's not dance."

Gerrett gently pulled her to the side so he could step past the curtained partition. He looked to the left and momentarily lost his ability to breathe. He couldn't move, couldn't think, couldn't do anything except listen to the frantic beat of his heart.

Liberty shifted her gaze from her glaring father to her glaring brother and back again. What had come over Leonidas? He had literally slapped the brandy snifter out of Father's hand, and the moment it had shattered on the floor, true to form, Caroline had fled the room.

"Leo," she said, "don't. This is neither the time nor place to…"

Her words died at the first tingle on the back of her neck. She could feel someone watching her, which was odd because they were in a room full of people. Anyone could be watching her. It wasn't just anyone she felt.

"Gerrett," she whispered.

She turned in her chair. All noise faded away. There he was, on the threshold of a private dining room. Not close enough to touch, yet her heart beat erratically. Gerrett cut a fine form in his tailored evening clothes, and with Ann in her ravishing beaded pink gown, they looked so beautiful together, it hurt.

When his gaze met Liberty's, he smiled, and she smiled, and he immediately took a step forward. Then he stopped, grabbed Ann Bartlett's elbow and—for all practical purposes—pulled her in their direction. Unlike Gerrett, Ann didn't look happy.

An odd sound emanated from Father.

Liberty turned back around. His gaze bore into her, and she wanted to shrink under the table. Years ago, when they had actually made attempts at being mother and daughter, she'd told Caroline of her feelings for Gerrett and swore her to secrecy. From the look Father was giving her, she knew Caroline had shared the news with him and now his mind was adding up information and calculating and calculating and calculating.

Liberty grabbed her brother's sleeve. "Gerrett and Ann are coming this way."

To her surprise, Leo didn't turn around to look. He pocketed the watch he'd set earlier on the table. "More's the merrier, I always say."

Father motioned to a waiter to bring him a replacement drink. He then placed his cigar in his mouth. "Where's your stepmother?"

"She fled," Liberty answered, hating the fact she hadn't come to Caroline's defense like Leonidas had. "You embarrassed her."

His upper lip twitched.

Gerrett stopped at the table, next to Leonidas, with Ann standing between Gerrett and Father.

"When did you return to Chicago?" Father blurted.

"Today, sir," Gerrett politely answered. His grip still stayed on Ann's elbow.

Leonidas leaned forward in his seat, and that devil-may-care glint in his eyes was back. "Father, Gerrett has been in Hillsdale for the past week."

Liberty gave her brother a swift kick, which he ignored.

"Is that so?" Father said, his interest in Gerrett clear. "Divine, what were you doing in Hillsdale?"

"I was stranded." He shrugged. "Train wreck. It was in all the papers."

If Liberty had any doubt as to her brother's feelings for Ann, they vanished upon seeing the desperate longing on his face as he gazed at her while Father questioned Gerrett about the wreck. Not once did Ann look Leonidas's way. Because she didn't share his feelings?

Liberty felt her mouth gape. Or because she did? *Oh, dear.*

Father laid his cigar on his plate and eyed Gerrett. "Divine, you didn't answer my question."

"Which was…?" Gerrett said with a casual grin.

"What were you *doing* in Hillsdale these past seven days?"

"Falling in love," Leonidas muttered.

At that, Ann tugged her arm from Gerrett's hold. "Yes, Gerrett, I will," she blurted in that clear melodic voice of hers. When Ann said anything, people listened not because she was demanding but because she was, well, undemanding. Practical. And so queenly as she spoke. Quite a fitting description considering she wore a triple-tiered pink taffeta gown that looked to be a Monsieur de Framboise design.

"You will what?" he answered, smiling.

"Marry you."

His expression lost all amusement. His voice lowered. "Why are you doing this?"

She released a soft chuckle. "I want children, and I know you will be a wonderful husband and father. As much as I yearn to chase after rapturous love, I choose to be practical because I need a man I can trust to be strong so I don't have to be."

Leonidas looked sick, wounded and, most of all, haunted.

Gerrett looked trapped.

Liberty wanted to cry. Or scream. Or do anything to stop this from happening. She wanted to help them, but how?

"So I ask," Ann said in a choked voice almost too low for Liberty to hear, "will you marry me?"

"I—" Gerrett started.

"Don't be so quick to answer," Father commanded. He paused as the waiter set his drink on the table then left. "Divine, have you fallen in love with my daughter?"

Liberty felt the blood drain from her face. Even in the dim lamplight, she was sure all could see how pale she'd grown. Thankfully, no one else in the dining hall was paying attention to their discussion. As she awaited Gerrett's answer to either question, Liberty glanced to her brother. He begged with his eyes what he had said to her earlier—*Stop the engagement.*

Please, he mouthed.

Should she? She enjoyed giving and serving and doing good for others.

Gerrett's eyes closed, his head bent. He was praying, that she knew, for direction. She wouldn't interfere. Whatever sifting God was doing in Gerrett's life, she had to step back and trust God to work it out for the best. Likewise, whatever sifting God was doing in Leonidas's life, she had to step back, too. He loved Ann. This was for him a possible Moment His Life Changed. He needed to let go of the fear holding him back. To seize his future. To pursue—*to choose*—the woman he loved.

He needed to do it for Ann.

He needed to do it for himself.

And the most loving thing she could do was not help him.

"No," she whispered.

Everyone, including Gerrett, looked her way.

"No, Divine doesn't love you?" Father asked.

Liberty blinked, momentarily speechless. "I have no idea if Gerrett loves me," she answered honestly. "He is my friend, and I am all right with that. Father, my *no* is for Leo alone."

He looked stunned.

She touched her brother's arm. "Because I have the ability to help doesn't mean I always have the responsibility. You need to do this. You *are* strong."

Leonidas turned from her to gaze openly at Ann, who looked ready to cry any moment.

"He needs to do what?" Father demanded. "Leonidas Aaron Judd, what is your sister talking about?"

Leonidas Judd loved Ann Bartlett. In a flash, Gerrett saw the list of evidence clearly in his mind.

Proof #1: The letters he'd received over the past year from Ann and Leonidas that had so many references to each other.

Proof #2: The fury Leonidas had exhibited at Gerrett's confession in Marseille that he had agreed to an arranged marriage with Ann. Gerrett had thought the response was directed to agreeing to an arranged marriage. Now he knew it'd been directed to the "with Ann" part.

Proof #3: Leonidas's fervent questioning at the train station that morning about what had occurred in Hillsdale, if Gerrett had seen Liberty and what his plans were for the evening.

Proof #4 (and the most convincing): The desperate longing in his friend's eyes.

Gerrett understood exactly how that felt. He also knew the pain he'd experienced when Liberty said she had no idea if he loved her. *I do,* he'd wanted to say. He was passionately, irrevocably in love with her. It was the strangest, grandest, most encompassing sensation. He should have recognized it himself before leaving Hillsdale. It was there all along, growing from the moment he'd seen her there in the snow.

And the joy from realizing it filled him with the knowledge that all would be well. Somehow. In his life. In hers. In Leonidas's and Ann's.

He wasn't going to question Liberty's arrival tonight. He suspected Leonidas had orchestrated their family being in this particular hotel, at this particular time, in this particular room. A man having gone to that much effort had a plan.

Plans stemmed from desires.

Gerrett did the only noble thing he could think of. He stepped aside, so he no longer stood between his two closest friends.

"Leo," he said, "do you have something you'd like to say to Ann?"

He'd never seen Leonidas tongue-tied.

Fingers curved around his, and he turned his head enough to the right to see Ann's blanched expression.

"Why are you doing this?" she whispered.

"I want children, and I know you will be a superb wife and mother. As much as I yearn to do the dutiful, practical and expected thing, I choose to be a romantic. You deserve a man who is in rapturous love with you." His hand cradled her cheek. "That's not me."

Leonidas's hands shook—from need for a drink or nerves, Gerrett wasn't sure—and he stayed silent. So did Ann. Yet the orchestra continued to play, and no one in the hotel restaurant gave much attention to Gerrett, Ann and the Judds.

Unable not to look at Liberty, Gerrett sought her eyes. She'd looked panicked earlier. Then hurt. Now she gazed at him, and the thread that connected them brought smiles to both their faces.

Mr. Judd cursed. "Will someone tell me what is going on?"

"Do it, Leo," Liberty prompted. She gave his arm a shove.

Leonidas stood. He stepped to Ann and took both of her hands in his. "Marry *me*. It doesn't have to be tomorrow. Or next month. Or even this year. I will wait as long as you need, but give me time to show you this God you keep telling me about has done something to my heart."

Nodding, Ann let out a choked sob.

Gerrett slid into Leonidas's empty seat and leaned toward Liberty. "Does this make you think of anything?" He did not touch her, because if he did, he didn't think he could stop.

She nodded. "Shakespeare."

"Shakespeare?"

"*Twelfth Night,* actually, a play I recently finished reading in my literature class."

"Ahh." He motioned with his head to Leonidas, who was escorting Ann to the private dining room where Gerrett's family still was. "Seems your brother has deprived me of a fiancée."

Liberty leaned forward, a smirk across her lips. "Seems you gave her away first."

"Seems I did."

"Are you pleased with that accomplishment?"

"Quite."

"Yes," Father abruptly announced. "Daughter, you have my approval."

Liberty's brow furrowed. "For?"

"You know what for." Mr. Judd massaged the corner of his mouth, Gerrett suspected, to hide a smile. "He'll do. Excuse me, I need to go find my wife and make amends." He nodded at Gerrett then walked off, leaving them at the table. Alone.

"I earned an A on my French exam," Liberty remarked.

Gerrett scooted his chair closer to hers, far enough for propriety, close enough to kiss, if he wanted. And he did. "You're smarter than you think you are."

"Some would say smarter than you."

"How is that, Miss Judd?"

She moistened her lips. "I have known for over seven years that I love you. How long did it take you to figure out you…love…me?"

He chuckled at that. "I'm in love with you?"

"Well, if I were making a list and tallying my conquests—" she eased to the edge of her chair "—you *are* the last addition, *and* the only one who has kissed me."

"How about you toss away that list and keep me?"

"Ahh. A girl could not receive a more romantic marriage proposal."

"Train car full of sarcasm, Miss Judd. Train car."

She curled her ankle around his. "Yes."

"Yes?"

"I'll keep you."

He considered extolling all the ways he loved her, but his lips descended on hers. Who knew a man could thank God for a train wreck.

Epilogue

"Gerrett Henry Divine, you come back here this instant!"

As the cuckoo clock downstairs rang the hour, Liberty snatched her red satin shoe out of the beagle's mouth then, flicking the slobber off the shoe, ran out of her bedroom after the adorable culprit, who had the matching one. If the shoes didn't perfectly match her gown—and these did—she would find another pair to wear.

"I will not let you ruin my graduation."

She stopped in the middle of the hall and swirled around. He was nowhere to be seen. The only other open door on this floor of the house was the spare room that she'd used during the past year as an office. She glanced inside. Next to her sewing machine was the basket of baby clothes she'd finished for Ann. Atop the small bed in the corner was a crate of college textbooks to give to Lady Principal Whipple. Four years of her life condensed into a crate. A dog bone and one of Gerrett's shoes lay next to the desk on the center rug.

She listened.

Not a sound.

He wouldn't have had time to run down the stairs without her seeing him, so the only other place on the floor someone of his size could be hiding—

She whirled around and tiptoed out of the room and back into the hall. At the end was a draped window seat; the curtains were drawn closed. The closer she walked, the greater her smile grew, to where her cheeks practically ached.

She heard the snicker first. Followed by a *shhh*. Then another snicker. She eased along the wall. Everyone would expect curtains to be parted from the middle, which was why she fingered an outer edge and drew it back.

"My shoe, please," she said sweetly.

His scream brought the dog running and barking.

Liberty covered her mouth to hide her smile.

"Shhh," Gerrett ordered, laughing. The dog quieted. So did Henry. "Looks like she found us, son."

Schooling her features, Liberty looked at her husband and two-year-old sitting on his scrunched-up lap. Henry clenched her shoe with both of his chubby hands. The mischievous tyke gave her his best repentant look…that she didn't believe for a moment. He was too much like his uncle.

"Don't you have a drawing to finish?" she asked Gerrett.

He scooped Henry into his arms then eased his legs out of the window seat and onto the floor. "Completed it while you dressed in that fetching red concoction that makes me think we should skip the graduation ceremony. A telegram arrived from Leonidas. Ann doubled our investments in the New Jersey iron mines, negotiated my contract to design the Milburn museum, then made it to the hospital in time to deliver a girl. Seven pounds, two ounces, with hair as black as her mother's."

"Did you buy—"

"Tickets to Chicago? We leave tomorrow." He stood and kissed her cheek. "They should give you a diploma for being the prettiest Hillsdale graduate."

"Thank you, Professor Divine."

"Teaching one architecture class doesn't make me a professor."

"I think it makes you wonderful." She wrapped her arms around him, and Henry laid his head against her shoulder. "Thank you," she whispered.

"What's the gratitude for?"

"Agreeing to live here in Hillsdale, not Chicago."

"Your father is more likable…from a distance."

She tipped her head to gaze up at him. "I love you, Mr. Divine. Frantically. Faithfully. Forever."

"Best thing I've heard all day, Mrs. Divine."

He kissed her. As the dog barked. As Henry discovered how to pull the pins out of her hair. As Liberty joyfully cleaved to him, even though she still thought *cleave* was the most ridiculous word she'd ever heard used in a sermon. Gerrett continued to kiss her even though she knew if he didn't stop, she would be late for her graduation. She was tempted to think he would continue to kiss her until they missed their train tomorrow.

He stopped when their son hit him with her shoe.

And then they laughed. All was right and good and perfect in their world, and in seven months, Liberty thought with a secret grin, it would be even more so.

* * * * *

REQUEST YOUR FREE BOOKS!

2 FREE INSPIRATIONAL NOVELS
PLUS 2
FREE
MYSTERY GIFTS

Love Inspired

YES! Please send me 2 FREE Love Inspired® novels and my 2 FREE mystery gifts (gifts are worth about $10). After receiving them, if I don't wish to receive any more books, I can return the shipping statement marked "cancel." If I don't cancel, I will receive 6 brand-new novels every month and be billed just $4.74 per book in the U.S. or $5.24 per book in Canada. That's a savings of at least 21% off the cover price. It's quite a bargain! Shipping and handling is just 50¢ per book in the U.S. and 75¢ per book in Canada.* I understand that accepting the 2 free books and gifts places me under no obligation to buy anything. I can always return a shipment and cancel at any time. Even if I never buy another book, the two free books and gifts are mine to keep forever.

105/305 IDN F49N

Name _____ (PLEASE PRINT) _____

Address _____ Apt. # _____

City _____ State/Prov. _____ Zip/Postal Code _____

Signature (if under 18, a parent or guardian must sign)

Mail to the Harlequin® Reader Service:
IN U.S.A.: P.O. Box 1867, Buffalo, NY 14240-1867
IN CANADA: P.O. Box 609, Fort Erie, Ontario L2A 5X3

**Are you a subscriber to Love Inspired books
and want to receive the larger-print edition?
Call 1-800-873-8635 or visit www.ReaderService.com.**

* Terms and prices subject to change without notice. Prices do not include applicable taxes. Sales tax applicable in N.Y. Canadian residents will be charged applicable taxes. Offer not valid in Quebec. This offer is limited to one order per household. Not valid for current subscribers to Love Inspired books. All orders subject to credit approval. Credit or debit balances in a customer's account(s) may be offset by any other outstanding balance owed by or to the customer. Please allow 4 to 6 weeks for delivery. Offer available while quantities last.

Your Privacy—The Harlequin® Reader Service is committed to protecting your privacy. Our Privacy Policy is available online at www.ReaderService.com or upon request from the Harlequin Reader Service.
We make a portion of our mailing list available to reputable third parties that offer products we believe may interest you. If you prefer that we not exchange your name with third parties, or if you wish to clarify or modify your communication preferences, please visit us at www.ReaderService.com/consumerchoice or write to us at Harlequin Reader Service Preference Service, P.O. Box 9062, Buffalo, NY 14269. Include your complete name and address.

LIDIR13R

REQUEST YOUR FREE BOOKS!

2 FREE INSPIRATIONAL NOVELS
PLUS 2
FREE
MYSTERY GIFTS

Love Inspired.
HISTORICAL
INSPIRATIONAL HISTORICAL ROMANCE

YES! Please send me 2 FREE Love Inspired® Historical novels and my 2 FREE mystery gifts (gifts are worth about $10). After receiving them, if I don't wish to receive any more books, I can return the shipping statement marked "cancel." If I don't cancel, I will receive 4 brand-new novels every month and be billed just $4.74 per book in the U.S. or $5.24 per book in Canada. That's a savings of at least 21% off the cover price. It's quite a bargain! Shipping and handling is just 50¢ per book in the U.S. and 75¢ per book in Canada.* I understand that accepting the 2 free books and gifts places me under no obligation to buy anything. I can always return a shipment and cancel at any time. Even if I never buy another book, the two free books and gifts are mine to keep forever.

102/302 IDN F5CY

Name	(PLEASE PRINT)	
Address		Apt. #
City	State/Prov.	Zip/Postal Code

Signature (if under 18, a parent or guardian must sign)

Mail to the Harlequin® Reader Service:
IN U.S.A.: P.O. Box 1867, Buffalo, NY 14240-1867
IN CANADA: P.O. Box 609, Fort Erie, Ontario L2A 5X3

Want to try two free books from another series?
Call 1-800-873-8635 or visit www.ReaderService.com.

* Terms and prices subject to change without notice. Prices do not include applicable taxes. Sales tax applicable in N.Y. Canadian residents will be charged applicable taxes. Offer not valid in Quebec. This offer is limited to one order per household. Not valid for current subscribers to Love Inspired Historical books. All orders subject to credit approval. Credit or debit balances in a customer's account(s) may be offset by any other outstanding balance owed by or to the customer. Please allow 4 to 6 weeks for delivery. Offer available while quantities last.

Your Privacy—The Harlequin® Reader Service is committed to protecting your privacy. Our Privacy Policy is available online at www.ReaderService.com or upon request from the Harlequin Reader Service.

We make a portion of our mailing list available to reputable third parties that offer products we believe may interest you. If you prefer that we not exchange your name with third parties, or if you wish to clarify or modify your communication preferences, please visit us at www.ReaderService.com/consumerschoice or write to us at Harlequin Reader Service Preference Service, P.O. Box 9062, Buffalo, NY 14269. Include your complete name and address.

LIHDIR13R

ReaderService.com

Manage your account online!
- Review your order history
- Manage your payments
- Update your address

---

*We've designed
the Harlequin® Reader Service
website just for you.*

Enjoy all the features!
- Reader excerpts from any series
- Respond to mailings and
  special monthly offers
- Discover new series available to you
- Browse the Bonus Bucks catalog
- Share your feedback

Visit us at:
ReaderService.com

RS13